D1058109

MORTAL TERM

MORTAL TERM

JOHN PENN

CHARLES SCRIBNER'S SONS
NEW YORK

First published in the United States by Charles Scribner's Sons 1985.

Copyright © John Penn 1984

Library of Congress Cataloging in Publication Data

Penn, John.
  Mortal term.

  1. Title.
PR6066.E496M6   1985   823'.914   84-23606
ISBN 0-684-18317-X

1 3 5 7 9 11 13 15 17 19 F/C 20 18 16 14 12 10 8 6 4 2

Printed in the United States of America.

Part One

After Term

CHAPTER 1

Hugh Roystone sweated gently as he made his way down St Aldate's. It was a hot summer afternoon in Oxford, and the sun beat up from pavements filled with shoppers and eager tourists. Traffic crowded the streets, threatening the pedestrians, the cyclists and the ancient buildings alike. Roystone was glad that he had been forced to leave the Headmasters' Conference before its end, immediately after the lunch following the delivery of his own paper. Though the meetings had taken place in his old college, he had not enjoyed them as much as in recent years. He'd not appreciated the sympathy of his colleagues, who had hastened to assure him that drug and sex problems were common to all schools. Nor had he welcomed inquiries after his wife, some of which he suspected were tinged with malice. He wondered how news of his recent ill fortune could have spread so quickly.

In any case, the ordeal, for such it had been, was over now; he was expected back at the school. Interviewing candidates for the posts that had fallen vacant was vastly more important than attending the final sessions of the conference, and the arrangements for the interviews had been made some time ago.

As soon as he reached his car—a pale grey Mercedes, slightly out of character for a nominally conservative headmaster, but one of his extravagances—Hugh Roystone flung his bag on the back seat, slipped off his jacket and loosened his tie. He took a deep breath, thankful that he would soon be out of the city and at home.

Hugh Roystone was a short, dark, thickset man, forty-one years old. An administrator rather than a scholar, with a pleasing personality, he had been headmaster of Coriston

College for the past six years. Coriston—pronounced 'Corston'—was not one of England's most prestigious independent public schools, and the fact that it ranked high in the second league was largely due to the influence of the headmaster. All such schools went through periods of fluctuating fortunes, and Coriston had been at a particularly low ebb when Roystone was appointed. Now, in spite of high fees, it had a waiting list and was preferred by a growing number of parents who approved of the homelike atmosphere of its boarding houses, as well as of its scholastic achievements. Until very recently, the Governors' choice of Hugh Roystone seemed to have been fully justified.

But the last term, the summer term—the Trinity Term as the school called it, following the practice of the nearby University of Oxford—had been disastrous. It had begun with high hopes, but ended miserably. Everything that could go wrong had gone wrong, Roystone thought bitterly, including his own marriage. As he drove up the Woodstock Road he wondered where Sylvia was now, what she was doing, and if she would ever come back to him. He swore softly under his breath.

Leaving the north Oxford by-pass, he turned on to the road that would take him to the country market town of Colombury, and then to Coriston, deeper in the heart of the Cotswolds. The bus from Oxford to Colombury followed the main road, through villages where there was a chance of passengers. He saw one ahead of him now, as he turned once more, this time on to the narrow and winding minor road that he always used. It was a toss-up which was the faster route—they often argued about it at Coriston—but at least this road was unfrequented and carried little traffic. In any case, it was Hugh Roystone's favourite.

Preoccupied with his thoughts, he didn't notice the girl until he was less than fifty yards from where she stood by the side of the road. She seemed to have materialized from nowhere, a slight figure—seemingly a mere child—in a short

pleated skirt, white blouse, white socks, carrying a straw
boater which she waved hesitantly.

Hitch-hikers were not uncommon in this part of the
country, and Roystone had no qualms about stopping. But
he was driving fairly fast, and he couldn't bring the Mercedes
to a halt until he was some distance beyond the girl. He
pushed his head out of the window and looked back, half
expecting to see her running after the car. But she merely
stood where she was, staring disconsolately at the cheap fibre
suitcase at her feet, her shoulders drooping.

Roystone backed up until he was level with her. 'Hello,' he
said. 'Where are you going? Do you want a lift?'

'Oh, sir, please. If you're going anywhere near
Colombury.'

'I am. Hop in.'

He opened the door for her and took her suitcase, turning
to put it on the back seat beside his bag. The girl climbed in
next to him. At close quarters he saw that she was older than
she had first appeared—thirteen, perhaps, or fourteen,
rather than ten or eleven. She had fair hair in two plaits, nice
blue eyes and a smudged face. It was obvious that she'd been
crying. Roystone smiled at her reassuringly.

'Do up your seat-belt.'

'Yes, sir. Thank you for stopping. One other car passed,
but it was full. A lorry driver did offer me a lift, but I didn't
think it was a good idea somehow.'

'You were quite right to be careful,' Roystone said
approvingly. 'What's your name?'

'Moira Gale, sir. And about what you said—about being
careful—I know. My mum'd be furious if she thought I was
begging lifts.'

'Then why are you?'

'I didn't have no choice.' Moira sniffed, produced a
grubby handkerchief and blew her nose. 'Someone nicked
my purse.'

'What?'

Roystone hid his grin. The child, woebegone as she looked, had sounded fierce and angry. He glanced sideways at her again. She was small-boned, fragile and quite appealing.

'It was like this,' she said. 'There's no direct way to get from Reading to Colombury, leastways not if you don't have a car. So I took the bus from Reading to Oxford. I was going to catch the afternoon bus on to Colombury, so I'd got time to get something to eat. Then I remembered I hadn't bought a gift for my auntie and I went into that big shop opposite the monument—'

'I know. It's Debenhams now.' Roystone supplied the name automatically. He had not been giving her story his full attention, but he said, 'So you're on your way to visit your aunt?'

'That's right. Her name's Gale too—Mrs Edna Gale. She married my dad's brother, but he died so she went back to live near her own family in Colombury. Her sister's Mrs Gotobed—the lady that runs the post office there. Perhaps you know them, sir, if you're from Colombury.'

'I'm not. I live in Coriston. That's some miles away.'

'Where the big school is? Are you a teacher, sir?'

'Yes. I'm the headmaster.'

'Oh!' Moira seemed slightly overawed. She bent forward and pulled up her socks.

'You were telling me why you were hitch-hiking,' Roystone said, hooting impatiently at a solitary Mini that was driving on the crown of the narrow road and preventing him from passing. 'You went to buy your aunt a present.'

'Yes. A scarf. My mum had given me the money. And that's where I lost my purse. I paid for the scarf, so I had it then, but I don't remember picking it up. The change was only a few pence and I put that in my blouse pocket. There were two ladies waiting to be served. I didn't want to keep them waiting any longer, and what with my case and my hat—' She left the sentence unfinished.

'But when you found your purse was missing, didn't you go back to the shop?' Roystone asked.

'Yes, I did, sir, but it wasn't there. The girl at the counter looked everywhere. She thought perhaps I'd dropped it in the street.'

'I see. So you were left without any money?'

'I had the bit of change left from buying my auntie's scarf, but it was only enough to get me a bus ride to the end of the Woodstock Road. Then I walked and tried to cadge a lift, but I didn't have any luck till you came along. I'd practically given up hope. I do thank you, sir.'

Her speech was a curious mixture of the uneducated and the stilted, Roystone reflected casually, as the girl turned in her seat and gave him a wide, tearful smile. She swallowed hard as if to stop herself crying again. And Hugh Roystone smiled back, touched by her obvious gratitude.

'Bloody road hog!' shouted Tom Ingle, the driver of the Mini, as Roystone overtook him. 'Just because he drives a big car he thinks he owns the place.'

'As if we didn't pay taxes too,' his mother agreed. 'We ought to have taken his number, reported him, we should. You didn't get it, did you, Rose?'

'No, I didn't, Ma.' Her daughter-in-law was squashed in the rear seat among innumerable sliding parcels. 'But I wish I had. That was dangerous driving, that was.'

The Mini continued through the Cotswolds at its ordained speed of thirty miles an hour. Old Mrs Ingle didn't like to be driven fast, and in any case three overweight people, together with all the things they'd bought in Oxford, put a severe strain on the Mini's capabilities, especially going uphill. Tom Ingle, who ran a butcher's shop in Colombury, could well have afforded a bigger car, but his mother decided all such matters and she liked what she called the 'cosiness' of the Mini.

The Ingles were on their way home after a trip to Oxford

and a lunch out to celebrate old Mrs Ingle's birthday. They'd enjoyed the opportunity to swear at Hugh Roystone, but they had no idea who he was. They didn't really expect to come across him again. Their malice was casual rather than personal.

Thus a few minutes later they were surprised to see the Mercedes stopped at the side of the road. It was one of the few straight stretches, running through a wood, and across the verge, on the grass where the trees began, a man was bending over a girl. Old Mrs Ingle grasped the scene first. In spite of her sixty-odd years her eyesight was excellent.

'Look!' she shouted. 'Look! Over there!'

'What are they doing?' Rose said.

'They seem to be—' Tom began.

But old Mrs Ingle knew what they were doing, or believed she knew. 'He's attacking that girl! He's trying to pull her into the trees. He's going to rape her, murder her. Quick, Tom! Step on it. We must get to her.'

It was to old Mrs Ingle's credit that without any thought for her own or her family's safety she urged her son to go to Moira Gale's rescue. Not that he needed any urging; he was no coward, and his mother didn't tell him to step on it very often. He jammed the accelerator to the Mini's floorboard, and the little car surged forward.

By now Roystone and Moira were struggling on the ground. Unintentionally Roystone gave the girl a glancing blow in the eye and, angry at the pain, she bit him hard in the fleshy part of the thumb. He had been trying to pinion her arms, to hold her still, but now he rolled off her, cursing.

Moira was on her feet immediately, screaming and waving her arms as she ran towards the approaching Mini. Her appearance told its own story. Her blouse was torn down the front, the buttons ripped off. The right shoulder strap of her bra was broken, and one small breast had an ugly graze across it. Her left eye was closed, and she sobbed hysterically as old Mrs Ingle, who had extracted herself from the interior of the Mini with surprising agility, rushed forward and enfolded her in a warm embrace.

'It's all right, dearie. You're all right now,' Mrs Ingle assured her comfortingly. 'We won't let the horrid man hurt you.'

'He tried—' Moira gasped. 'He wanted me to lie down and—Oh God, he's coming!' She buried her face in Mrs Ingle's capacious bosom, and clung to her like a small child. 'Help me, please.'

Mrs Ingle was never one to miss a moment of drama. 'Not to worry, dearie,' she said, thrusting Moira behind her as Hugh Roystone came striding towards them. He'd got to his feet, brushed himself down and fought to control his feelings. Now he was ready to deal with the situation.

He found himself faced by the three of them—old Mrs Ingle, her son and her daughter-in-law. They stood in front of their Mini, almost shoulder to shoulder, the girl behind them. They looked ludicrous, but Roystone had no desire to laugh. He was cold with anger, both against himself and against the girl.

Tom Ingle took a step forward. 'What do you want, mister? You've caused enough trouble, by the looks of it.'

'You're a dirty old man,' Mrs Ingle intervened boldly, ignoring the fact that Roystone was at least twenty years her junior.

Hugh Roystone glared at her. 'I don't know what the girl's been saying, but—'

'She didn't need to tell us nothing, poor dear. We saw it all for ourselves,' Tom Ingle said. 'If we'd not come along when we did you'd have had her, and probably killed her afterwards. That's what the likes of you do, mister. You're a menace. You ought to be in prison. I've said so before and I'll say it again, people like you ought to be shut up—'

'And we're going to see you are,' his mother said firmly. 'This little girl's all right now, but if we don't do something he'll be after another. Who are you? What's your name?'

Roystone had been containing his temper with difficulty. Now it exploded. 'Don't be so bloody silly!' he said. 'I didn't lay a finger on the girl. She—' He stopped, seeing the utter disbelief on their faces. He turned on his heel. 'To hell with you!'

Tom Ingle started forward as if to attempt to tackle Roystone, but old Mrs Ingle put a restraining grip on her son's arm.'It doesn't matter, mister,' she shouted. 'We've got your number and we know what you look like. The police'll do what's necessary. They'll find you all right.'

Breathing hard, Roystone strode back to his car. Nothing he could say would convince them. The stupid dolts were beyond reason. They thought they knew it all. Anyway, why should he care what they thought?

Reaching the Mercedes, he seized Moira Gale's suitcase and flung it on to the grass verge, glad when it burst open and scattered its contents. Let her three fat friends pick up her things for her, he thought irrationally. The little bitch! He got into the car, flung the girl's straw hat after the suitcase, and started the engine.

It was only then, as he settled himself in the driving seat, that he realized his fly was unzipped and part of his shirt hanging out of his trousers. Suddenly he felt sick and ashamed. This was the end—the culmination of a trail of misfortune that had begun on the first day of the summer term.

Part Two

Term Time

CHAPTER 2

The summer term at Coriston College had begun on a grey, rainy day late the previous April. From about ten o'clock in the morning to six o'clock in the evening a succession of cars had driven through the wrought-iron gates and up the long tree-lined drive to deliver pupils to one or other of the six boarding houses—three for boys and three for girls—scattered through the grounds. Trains, full of chattering boys and girls laden with luggage and sports equipment, had been met at Oxford and Colombury stations. Coriston, so quiet for the last few weeks, had come alive again.

Unless they had special permission to arrive late, all the pupils had to be in the school by five-thirty. The heads of the boarding houses—there were four married housemasters in the school and two unmarried housemistresses—all naturally lived on the job, as it were, in the houses for which they were responsible. Together with their respective staffs they had been busy all day, welcoming pupils, greeting any parents who were in evidence, and escorting a favoured few to call on the headmaster. But by half past eight, there was relative peace. Supper was over, and the younger children were getting ready for bed. The older ones were in their studies. At least that was the theory.

Because it was the first night of term a certain amount of licence was allowed. There was a lot of coming and going between studies and common rooms, sudden bursts of noise, an occasional boisterous act that ended in some minor disaster. But staff kept out of the way, and prefects turned a blind eye. Tomorrow the excitement of meeting old friends and old enemies after the Easter break would have subsided. The term would begin in earnest.

It was the custom for Hugh Roystone, as headmaster, to

entertain his senior staff—mainly the heads of houses and their wives—to coffee and liqueurs on this, the first evening of term. It was a time to relax after a hard day. It was pleasant—and sometimes useful—to sit about, talking shop and exchanging gossip, in an informal atmosphere. And this particular party had an added attraction—Roystone's new young wife.

The headmaster of Coriston College had an apartment in a wing of what was known as College House. No children were housed there, but it was the centre of school activity and where most of the actual teaching took place. College House was in fact the original Coriston Hall, a great Georgian mansion once the seat of the Coriston family, long since extinct. The headmaster's apartment was not large, but it was elegant and recently refurbished. The sitting-room was looking its best tonight, curtains drawn against the dismal evening, lights on and a log fire burning on the hearth.

Helen Quarry, the wife of the deputy headmaster and senior housemaster, went across to her husband, who was chatting to the school secretary, Frances Bell. Helen and Frances were old friends, though very dissimilar in character. They were both in their early forties, but Helen was a big, warm, motherly woman—an ideal wife for the head of a girls' boarding house. Frances, on the other hand, was small, dark and super-efficient with an acid tongue. As Helen came up behind her Frances abruptly stopped speaking.

John Quarry laughed. 'It's okay, Frances. Only Helen.'

'Thanks be for that.' Unusually for her, Frances Bell gave a sheepish grin. 'I was being horribly uncharitable. But really, Helen, if our revered headmaster had to marry someone half his age, he might at least have chosen someone—well, someone more suitable.' :

The three of them studiously avoided looking towards Sylvia Roystone, who was standing by the fire and listening to Mark Joyner, the most junior of the housemasters. The new—very new—Mrs Roystone was a pretty girl, fair, blue-eyed, slim, and quite clearly completely out of her element. In the first place, she was at least ten years younger than anyone else in the room. Then, while everyone else had discarded the gowns and formal attire in which they'd earlier greeted parents and pupils for more casual clothes, Sylvia Roystone was over-dressed, in black silk with pearls at her throat and in her ears. Perhaps it was because she was embarrassed by her misjudgement that she had so little to say for herself.

'She's certainly more than half Hugh's age,' Helen Quarry protested mildly.

'There's seventeen years between them.' Frances Bell was firm. 'And she's so diffident, so unsure of herself.'

'I expect she's shy,' Helen said. 'It can't be easy for her, coming to a place like Coriston, and being pitchforked into this sort of party. Worse than meeting one's in-laws for the first time.'

Frances shrugged. 'To my mind, she's not what you expect of a headmaster's wife.'

'Unfortunately headmasters aren't always chosen for their wives, though God knows what they are chosen for sometimes.' There was bitterness in John Quarry's voice. He glanced towards Sylvia Roystone. 'I think I'll go and talk to her. Poor Mark's done his duty for long enough. He's beginning to look a bit glazed.'

Nodding to his wife and Frances Bell, Quarry sauntered across to the drinks table. He helped himself to another brandy and stood for a moment surveying the gathering. A tall, good-looking man—had he not been so gaunt he might have been described as handsome—his expression was sardonic. Then, shrugging, he went across to Sylvia Roystone and Mark Joyner.

Joyner was obviously glad to see him. 'Hello, John. I was just telling Mrs Roystone that I'm still two boys short in my house. You can guess the ones who haven't turned up yet.'

'Pierson and Grey?'

'Right! If it had been anyone else—any other couple—I'd have been phoning their families and hoping that nothing disastrous had happened. But not with these two. They think rules are only there to be bent or broken.' Mark Joyner grinned cheerfully. 'Not even making them house prefects changed them, though I must admit they're good with the younger boys.'

'The buggers should have had their arses tanned years ago,' John Quarry said.

'Er—yes.' Joyner threw an anxious glance at the girl beside them, wondering how she would take this remark. Then he seized his opportunity. 'If you'll excuse me . . .'

'I hope I didn't shock you, Mrs Roystone?' Quarry said as Joyner left them. 'I get rather tired of friends Pierson and Grey.'

Sylvia Roystone flushed. 'No, no.' There was an awkward silence and she added quickly, 'Actually, I—I think Hugh said there isn't any corporal punishment at Coriston.'

'*Corston!*' Quarry corrected her with unnecessary sharpness. 'Spelt Coriston but pronounced *Corston*.'

Sylvia Roystone's flush deepened. 'Oh, of course. I know. I just forgot. I'm sorry.'

Quarry smiled, waving away her excuses as if she were one of his less intelligent pupils. 'You're quite right. Your husband abolished corporal punishment when he came here. I'm sure you'd agree his decision was right. Certainly when I was at school bare bottoms always brought out the baser instincts in masters and pupils alike.'

'John!' Helen Quarry interrupted.

The word conveyed only the faintest of warnings, but there was no doubt about the meaning of Helen's grip on her husband's arm. His smile widened and he gently released himself, making his escape as Hugh Roystone came up with Lyn Joyner.

Smiling affectionately at his young wife, Roystone said, 'Darling, Lyn's just promised to give you some tennis coaching. Isn't that kind of her? I told her you could be quite good if you worked at it, though I'm afraid you'll have a job to beat her. She plays for the county.' He patted Sylvia on the shoulder and left the three women.

'It's awfully kind of you, but—' Sylvia began hesitantly.

'I should enjoy it, really. Before I married Mark I used to be a games mistress. You've never been a teacher, have you?'

'No.' It was a flat monosyllable.

Lyn Joyner looked at the younger woman curiously. She herself was always full of energy and enthusiasm, and she felt rebuffed by Sylvia Roystone's obvious reserve. 'What did you do?' she asked. 'You must have finished with university.'

'I never went to a university.'

'Nor did I,' Helen Quarry intervened. 'Except briefly. I met John in my first year, and that was that as far as higher education went. In fact, I'm a drop-out. But I've no regrets.'

Lyn took the hint. 'Who would if they were married to your John?' she said. She waved a hand and drifted away.

The noise level in the room had risen by several decibels and Sylvia's voice was soft. Helen had to lean towards her to hear what she was saying.

'. . . actually, I—I left school at sixteen. My parents had separated and married again, and somehow I didn't fit in with either family. I went to live with an aunt. She died just before Easter.'

'This year? As recently as that?'

'Yes.'

'I see.' In her own mind, Helen filled in the gaps in Sylvia's story. 'And then you married Hugh,' she said.

Sylvia's face lit up. 'Yes. He was wonderful. He coped with everything.' She stopped, momentarily embarrassed, but Helen Quarry invited confidences. 'My aunt and I always spent Christmas at hotels, and I met Hugh at one last December. We wrote to each other a lot afterwards, and when he heard my aunt had died he—he came at once. But I expect he's told you all this.'

Helen didn't answer directly. In fact, Hugh Roystone had told them very little. He had been uncharacteristically secretive, and the marriage had come as a complete surprise to his colleagues and friends. None of them had been asked to the wedding. An announcement in *The Times* less than a week ago was the first time anyone had heard Sylvia's name, and this party was the first occasion on which most of the senior staff had had any opportunity to meet their headmaster's new wife. Naturally the details of the sudden romance had been the subject of intensive speculation. Everyone had believed that at over forty Hugh Roystone was a confirmed bachelor, and an exception to the rule that headmasters should preferably be married.

Helen said, 'My dear, I hope you'll be very happy. If—if there are any difficulties in the school—and I expect there will be—remember that I've a daughter very little younger than you.' Spontaneously she put an arm round Sylvia and hugged her for a moment.

'Thank you. Thank you very much,' Sylvia said. Then she lifted her head. 'Was that the telephone? I'd better answer it.'

But Frances Bell was already on her way to take the call in the headmaster's study, which led off the sitting-room. It didn't occur to the efficient school secretary not to answer the phone herself. Now Hugh was married, she wouldn't have considered going into any other part of the Roystones' apartment—to telephone or for any other reason—without invitation, but she looked upon the study and the adjoining office as her own domain.

There was a lull in the conversation as she came back to the party. She said, 'That was your house, Mark. Your missing lambs have been found! Pierson and Grey are at Colombury station. They were helping an old lady with her luggage, and the train they should have caught left without them.'

Her announcement was greeted with derisory laughter

from almost everyone. Mark Joyner was an exception, and
he exchanged resigned glances with his wife. The boys were
from his house, and his responsibility.

'And now they're waiting to be fetched, I suppose,' he
said.

'That's right,' Frances agreed. 'They've been trying to get
a lift, but no one seems to be coming Coriston way.'

'Why not let them walk, Mark?' someone suggested.

'They wouldn't. I bet they'd spend the night living it up at
the Windrush Arms—as far as you can live anything up
in Colombury—and phone again in the morning.' Joyner
shook his head, doing his best to make a joke of the incident. 'There's nothing for it. I'll have to go and get the
wretches.'

'I'll go!'

The room was suddenly still. Everyone had turned to
Sylvia Roystone, their faces smiling but startled.

'It's very kind of you,' Mark Joyner began, 'but—'

'Of course you can't go, darling,' Hugh Roystone said.

'Of course not! You don't even know the boys.' Whereas
Roystone's objection had been casual, Lyn Joyner was
positive, brushing aside the suggestion. 'Mark must go.'

'Nonsense!' Colour flamed in Sylvia's cheeks. 'You've all
been working hard all day, and I've been doing nothing. At
least let me help when I can. I've got a bit of a headache and
I'd enjoy the drive. I know where Colombury station is, and
I'm sure I can find two boys. What are they called? Pierson
and Grey?'

'Tony Pierson and Peter Grey.' Joyner hesitated. 'It's
awfully good of you. I'm tired, I know, but—it is my job.' He
looked at Roystone questioningly; it was for the headmaster
to decide.

'Sylvia, it's not a particularly nice night, you know. Do
you really want to go? Shall I come with you?' Roystone
said.

'No, you can't leave your guests. And I do want to go. The

air'll do me a lot of good. I'll just get my coat. But I don't
know how long I'll be, so perhaps I'd better say, "Good-night
everyone".'

There was a chorus of good-nights and thank-yous as
Sylvia Roystone left. Sylvia's suggestion seemed to have
become a *fait accompli*. Her husband went with her as far as
the door of the apartment. He took her by the shoulders and
looked at her, momentarily anxious.

'Darling, you're sure you'll be all right? You're not just
doing this to get out of the rest of the party, are you?' he asked
gently. 'They'll be going soon, you know. They won't stay
late. Tomorrow's a working day. Then we can go straight
to bed and I'll bring you some milk and an aspirin or
something. The maids'll do all the clearing up in the
morning.'

'Hugh, I'm not trying to get out of anything. As I said, I'd
just like some fresh air to clear my head. I'll be quite all right,
and I shan't be very long. I'll see you soon, darling.' Sylvia
spoke hurriedly, perhaps too hurriedly.

'Okay then. Take care.' Hugh's lips brushed hers.
'Remember, I love you.'

Smiling to himself, Hugh Roystone returned to his colleagues. He was a contented man, he reflected, one of the
happiest men alive.

CHAPTER 3

Sylvia Roystone hurried along the corridor and down a flight
of stairs. She was now in College House proper. The area was
well lit, but there was an empty, eerie feeling about it, and
she pulled her coat more closely around her. Her footsteps
echoed. She had forgotten to change her shoes and was still
wearing high-heeled, open-toed sandals.

'I say! Hi, there!'

Startled, Sylvia turned and almost tripped on the bottom step, only saving herself by grabbing the handrail. A man was running down the stairs behind her, waving an umbrella. He was young, she saw as he reached her, about her own age, tall, with untidy fair hair and a pleasant, open face. He grinned at her.

'I'm terribly sorry. I didn't mean to frighten you.'

'That's all right.' Sylvia returned his smile. 'I didn't expect anyone to be in this part of the building at this time.'

'I probably shouldn't be here. But I only arrived this afternoon and I wanted to see the language lab before tomorrow. I found the way there, but when I came to leave I couldn't get out by the door I got in by, if you see what I mean. Someone must have locked it while I was having a look at the equipment. I found another door, but I got myself lost. I hope you'll show me how to get out of the building. I don't want to spend the night here. It would be horribly uncomfortable . . .' The young man's voice trailed away as he looked at Sylvia Roystone in mock appeal.

'Of course I will. It's very confusing, I know.'

They began to walk along a broad corridor together. Sylvia was conscious of being regarded appraisingly, and she had to bite her bottom lip to prevent herself from returning his gaze.

'I ought to introduce myself,' he said at length. 'I'm Steve Leyton, the new assistant language master. Very new and very assistant. To be honest, it's my first job ever, and I'm only on probation at the moment. Whether I stay depends on how well I do. It's a bit off-putting, isn't it? Anyway, I think it is.' He answered his own question. 'But how about you? Have you been here long? You can't have been. You're too young. What do you teach? More important, which house are you in? I'm in Joyner's.'

Steve Leyton's high spirits and his style of conversation were infectious, and Sylvia didn't attempt to hide her amusement. She turned and laughed up at him, saying, 'I'll try and answer all those questions, just for you. I'm not in anyone's house. I don't teach anything. I've been here at Coriston for about two weeks, so I'm almost as new as you are.'

'Okay! Don't tell me any more! I know,' Leyton said. 'You must be a matron—Mrs Cole's assistant—or you're a Cordon Bleu and all that, and you're going to cope with our food.'

'No, it's nothing like that. I'm Sylvia Roystone.'

For a moment the penny didn't drop. Then Leyton exclaimed, 'Oh Christ! The head's new wife! And here I am chatting her up as if—'

'Please! It doesn't matter in the least,' Sylvia protested. 'It makes no difference.'

'It most certainly does, Mrs Roystone, if you'll forgive me for contradicting you.'

Steve Leyton gave a little bow. He stopped walking as he overplayed his agitation, and Sylvia was forced to stop too. They stood facing each other. He said, 'Alas, it's not permitted for one in my lowly position to be chums with the headmaster's wife, and I certainly couldn't ask her for a date.'

Sylvia regarded him doubtfully, unsure whether or not he was serious. She opened her mouth to reply, but the sound of a door closing and voices in a side corridor made her pause. Then around the corner came an attractive couple, both seemingly in their early thirties, a man of medium height whose spectacles concealed an intelligent and interesting face, and a woman in a tight skirt and sweater that drew attention to her figure.

'Hello, Steve,' the man said. 'What are you doing here?'

Leyton explained rapidly. 'Mrs Roystone was kindly showing me the way out of this place,' he said. 'Er—you do know Mrs Roystone?'

'No. We've not met,' the woman said, 'but of course we've heard the happy news.'

Waving a hand, Leyton introduced the couple. 'Paula

Darby who teaches English, and Simon Ford. He's maths. I met them both this afternoon.'

'Mrs Roystone?' Ford made no attempt to conceal his interest in Sylvia. He inspected her face and figure carefully, if perhaps a little sardonically. 'Our headmaster has excellent taste, if I may say so, Mrs Roystone. He's to be congratulated.'

'Thank you,' Sylvia said, smiling. 'I think I'm very lucky too.'

'You're wearing a coat. Are you on your way out? Not far, I hope. It's a horrid night.'

'I'm picking up some boys from Colombury station. They missed the earlier train.'

'*You* are?' Ford didn't bother to hide his surprise.

Once again Sylvia tried to explain. '. . . I just wanted the fresh air, and it's not really far.'

'I don't envy you,' Paula Darby said. 'The minibus drives like a tank and on wet roads in the dark it's no joke.'

Sylvia frowned. 'No one said anything about a minibus. I was going to take my own car. I don't have a key for the minibus.'

'The key's no problem,' Ford said. 'It's always left in the ignition. We're all secretly hoping someone will steal the thing. But it's absurd you should be doing this. Surely someone else would—'

'Yes, of course. I'll go,' Leyton said at once. 'How many boys are there and where do I pick them up?'

Sylvia Roystone shook her head firmly. 'Thank you, but no. I said I'd go and I'm going. But there are only two boys and it never occurred to me I wouldn't take my own car.'

'They'll have trunks and tennis rackets and all sorts of gear,' Paula Darby reminded her. 'Unless you've got a big car you don't care about I'd suggest you take the minibus, Mrs Roystone, brute though it is.'

'Or take up Steve's offer. That's what I'd advise. Or let him come with you,' Ford said.

'No. I'm going by myself, as I said. But not in my car. It's new. Hugh gave it to me as a wedding present and I wouldn't like the upholstery messed up.'

'How nice!' There was an edge of sarcasm in Paula Darby's voice.

'Yes, if you had to marry a schoolmaster, you were lucky to find one with a private income,' Ford said. There was a hint of malice behind the words though he was laughing as he spoke. 'Anyway, if you're really determined, okay. But at least let us show you where the minibus is. And Steve's got an umbrella.'

In fact, the rain had ceased for the moment, and they could easily pick their way around the side of College House to what had originally been the stables. The minibus stood in the yard.

The three of them—Paula Darby, Ford and Leyton—regarded Sylvia doubtfully as she climbed into the bus, but she started the engine and moved off without apparent difficulty. In fact, she was an excellent driver. She had acted as her aunt's chauffeur and before that pernickety woman—the elder sister of Sylvia's mother—had entrusted herself to her niece she had seen to it that the girl was an expert. It was one of the few accomplishments for which Sylvia had reason to thank her aunt.

The minibus was old, the seat uncomfortable, the steering heavy and the gears difficult, but Sylvia had no problems. She drove out of the yard and down the drive at a steady pace. As she reached the main gates the rain started again, first as a drizzle, then a steady downpour. Sylvia glanced at her watch. The weather might delay her, but it was an easy road to Colombury and there should be little traffic. She should be at the station in about thirty minutes.

An hour later Tony Pierson telephoned the school again, and this time spoke directly to his housemaster. No one, he complained, had come to pick them up. The two of them—Peter Grey and himself—were cold and hungry. They wanted to know what they should do. Mark Joyner was not sympathetic. He said that Mrs Roystone had gone to fetch them. Where had they been? How had they come to miss her?

'We haven't moved from the station, sir. I swear it,' Pierson said. 'And we've been watching for a car, any car, because we weren't sure who was coming for us. We don't know the head's new wife, of course, but honestly, sir, she can't have been here or we'd have seen her.'

'All right. I believe you.'

'You don't think she's had an accident, do you?'

'I hope to God not!' Mark Joyner made up his mind quickly. 'Tony, you and Peter stay where you are. I'll be leaving here in five minutes. If Mrs Roystone turns up before I get to you, go with her and look out for me on the way. You know my car. Right?'

'Yes, sir. Thank you, sir. We're sorry about all this.'

'So you damn well should be.' Joyner, in shirt and under-pants, slammed down the receiver by his bedside and turned to his wife, sitting at her dressing-table. 'You gathered what that was about?'

'Yes. But what do you think's happened to Mrs R?'

'Oh, I expect she's lost her way,' Joyner said irritably. 'It's my own fault. I should have gone myself, but she was so insistent.'

'Don't feel guilty about it, sweetie. She certainly wanted to go and Hugh didn't try very hard to stop her. Incidentally, he'll have to be told.'

'Yes, I suppose so. Damn it!' Mark Joyner finished strug-gling into his clothes and looked hopefully at Lyn. 'Will you call him?'

'Okay,' she said reluctantly.

'Bless you.' Joyner gave her a quick kiss on the mouth and hurried out of their bedroom.

Lyn Joyner wasted no time. At once she dialled the headmaster's number on the internal phone system and, when Roystone answered, told him that Mark had gone to fetch the two boys as Mrs Roystone hadn't yet arrived at the station. Of course, Mark would keep a sharp lookout for her on the way. She tried to make light of the matter, and said she was sure there was no need to worry.

'Probably she took a wrong turning and got lost,' Lyn said. 'Or perhaps she's had a flat tyre. We'll hear soon.'

'Yes, of course,' Roystone agreed. 'Thanks, Lyn.'

Slowly Roystone put down the phone, his brow creased in a frown. Useless to say not to worry. How could he help worrying? Sylvia was a more than competent driver and the route from Coriston to Colombury was straightforward. She should have been at the station ages ago. Something must have happened.

He was turning away from the telephone to consider his next move when it rang, and he snatched up the receiver. 'Hugh Roystone here,' he said quickly.

'Hugh, it's me—Sylvia.'

'Thank God! Where are you, darling? Are you all right?'

'I'm at Colombury police station. Please come, Hugh. I've had an accident.'

'Accident? Are you hurt?'

'No! But I—' Over the phone her quick intake of breath sounded like a sob.

'Sylvia, for heaven's sake, what—'

'Just come, Hugh! Please!'

Hugh Roystone found his wife in a small, cheerless room at the rear of Colombury police station—the only so-called interview room in the building. She was sitting at a wooden table, apparently totally oblivious of the young uniformed policewoman in a corner. Sylvia's arms were clasped around her body as if to stop herself from shivering. She was very pale. She glanced up as he came in, but showed no sign of welcome.

'Sylvia, darling, it's all right. I'm here now. I've come to take you home. Everything's all right.'

'No.' Sylvia shook her head, and tears began to trickle down her cheeks. Hugh started forward.

'It's best if she cries, sir.' The policewoman got to her feet, smiling sympathetically. 'Get her to tell you what happened, sir, and let her cry. I'll make you a cup of tea, and another one for Mrs Roystone. Perhaps she'll drink it now you're here. It'd be good for her.'

'Thanks,' Roystone replied absently, willing the girl to go and leave them alone. 'That's kind of you.' As soon as the door shut behind her he knelt down beside Sylvia and gathered her to him as if she were a child. He rocked her gently, whispering endearments, until she broke down and wept unrestrainedly, clinging to him fiercely. He wiped her face with his handkerchief. Then, the policewoman having returned with two large earthenware mugs of tea, he persuaded his wife to drink some.

'I'm sorry,' she said. 'I'm sorry, Hugh.'

'Darling, everyone has an accident sooner or later if they drive long enough. The main thing is that you're not hurt. It doesn't matter about the car or—or anything else. I'm going to take you home now and put you to bed. You've had a shock. We'll get the doctor to give you something if necessary.'

'It wasn't my car, Hugh. I took the school minibus because of the boys' luggage. Perhaps if it had been my car and I'd changed my shoes. But my foot slipped off the brake and—and—' Sylvia couldn't continue.

'You took the minibus?' Roystone swallowed his surpise. But Sylvia had buried her face in her hands and he put his arms round her again, lifting her to her feet. 'Come on, darling. We'll sort it all out tomorrow. Now you're going home.'

'If you wouldn't mind waiting a couple of minutes, sir,' the policewoman interrupted.

Roystone had temporarily forgotten her presence. 'Why?' he demanded.

'The statement, sir. It's being typed. It's almost ready and if Mrs Roystone could sign it before she goes, she—'

'Statement? What statement? Mrs Roystone's in no condition to make any statement. Surely you can see that?' Roystone was angry. 'If she's said anything and you've taken it down, you can forget it as a statement. She's signing nothing tonight.'

'But—' The policewoman was taken aback at his vehemence. Luckily at that moment the door of the interview room opened and a sergeant came in carrying some pages of typescript. 'Sir,' the girl said, 'this is Sergeant Court.'

'I know Sergeant Court.' Roystone nodded. A year or so ago there had been an outbreak of vandalism in the college grounds, and Court had managed to apprehend the local youths who were responsible. 'I saw him when I came in, but he said nothing about a statement. Sergeant, what's all this nonsense about making my wife give a statement?'

'No one made her, sir. It was quite voluntary, and in my opinion a wise thing to do. After all, when a child's involved like that—'

'Like what? What child? You didn't mention any child—or any statement—just now.'

Sergeant Court refrained from commenting that he'd had no chance to say anything when Roystone arrived. The headmaster had stormed into the police station, demanding to see his wife immediately. He'd not been prepared to listen to any explanations from anyone. Wordlessly Court handed him the typescript.

It was in reality quite short, and Roystone read it quickly. 'I was driving at about thirty miles an hour . . . it was raining . . . the street lights shone on puddles in the road . . . the little boy suddenly appeared in front of me . . . I braked hard but I wasn't used to the minibus . . . I'd never driven it before and I was wearing high-heeled sandals . . . my foot slipped . . . I couldn't stop in time . . . I felt the wheel go over him . . . it was like hitting a—a branch . . .'

'Is the child badly hurt?' Roystone asked bleakly.

'I'm afraid so, sir, yes, though we don't know how badly yet. The ambulance has taken him to Oxford. Fortunately for Mrs Roystone, there was a witness who said the boy just ran into the road. There shouldn't be any trouble, unless—'

'Unless he dies,' Sylvia Roystone said. 'Then I shall have killed him.'

CHAPTER 4

The College's indoor swimming pool was new—the result of an Old Coristonians' appeal—and it was housed in a building of its own. At seven o'clock in the morning it was empty, which was how Hugh Roystone liked it. In less than half an hour the pool would echo to the voice of the coach as he spurred on aspirants for the Coriston team to greater efforts. Now all was quiet and peaceful, except for the slap of water against the tiles as Roystone turned at the far end to swim his final length at a fast crawl.

He reached his goal and heaved himself out of the water. Leaving damp footprints on the tiles, he went off to the showers. Burning hot, then icy cold, he let the needles of water bounce off his skin. He pulled on a track suit and was ready to leave as the swimming hopefuls arrived for their session. Acknowledging their chorus of 'Good morning, sir', he jogged unhurriedly back to College House.

Usually at this time he felt both relaxed and invigorated. He'd always enjoyed his pre-breakfast swim. But in the three weeks that had passed since Sylvia's accident everything had changed. Everything. The entire school seemed to have been infected. There was more than usual 'naughtiness'—even some quite unpleasant incidents—among the juniors, unusual insolence among those who would be leaving at the end of term, outbreaks of bullying and ragging, complaints from the staff, behaviour he could only describe as irrational. It was a poor beginning to the Trinity Term.

Hugh Roystone sighed as he opened the door to College House. His biggest problem, he knew, was Sylvia. She maintained that there was nothing wrong with her, but she remained listless and withdrawn. She refused to take any part in the social life of the school, but merely went for long solitary walks, or sat alone in the small walled garden that was reserved for the headmaster. Otherwise she hardly left the apartment. She read a lot, and every day she telephoned the hospital.

There was no news of the little boy's progress, though they now knew quite a lot about him. His name was Billy Morton and he was six. He had been returning from a visit to his aunt with his mother and his elder brother, Greg, when he'd seen his father come out of the Windrush Arms on the other side of the main street in Colombury. Pulling free of his mother's hand he had dashed over to meet him. Hence, the accident. The boy had been in a coma ever since.

Except to say, when asked, that there was no change, Sylvia rarely spoke of the boy. Indeed, it seemed to Hugh that she didn't speak much about anything, and this morning as he'd swum one length of the pool after another he'd reached a decision. The Quarrys had asked them to dinner that evening—just them, not a party. He hadn't yet told Sylvia, but he was determined they should go.

She had been asleep when he left. Now he took her an early morning cup of tea, and sat on the bed beside her. She drank it obediently, like a child, but with no sign of pleasure.

He said, 'Darling, we're having dinner tonight with Helen and John. I know you'll say you don't want to go, but we're going. It's important that we should. There'll only be the four of us, and they're good friends of ours.'

'Of yours.'

'And yours. Helen especially. You must admit she couldn't have been kinder or more understanding over this business.'

'Kind and understanding? You mean she's a nice woman and so she's sorry for me. But in her heart she blames me, like everyone else. Why shouldn't she? How can she help it? I blame myself.'

'Sylvia, darling, we've been over this time after time. It was an accident. You know it was.'

'But it need never have happened, Hugh! I should never have taken that minibus. I should have gone in my own car; the boys' luggage could have followed the next day, if necessary. If only I'd been in my car, if only I'd thought to change my shoes, if my reactions had been quicker, if—Then little Billy—' Sylvia's voice broke.

'For Christ's sake!' Hugh Roystone rarely swore. 'What on earth's the point of all these "ifs"? It wasn't your fault the child ran across the street when he did.'

'It was my fault I didn't stop sooner.'

Roystone shook his head in exasperation. 'All right, Sylvia, if you say so,' he said. 'But we're still dining with the Quarrys tonight.'

'I shouldn't go to too much trouble if I were you, Helen,' John Quarry said. 'I bet you anything they cry off at the last minute.'

'No. Hugh was quite definite about it. They'll come. And we can't give them ordinary school food.'

'Okay, but don't be too extravagant.' Quarry shrugged into his black gown and picked up a pile of papers and exercise books. 'See you later, love.'

Smiling to herself, Helen Quarry went along to her little kitchen. She enjoyed cooking and was glad of an excuse to prepare a special meal. An hour later, enveloped in a large blue and white striped apron, she was completely absorbed, humming as she worked with the electric mixer whirring loudly. She failed to hear the knock on the green baize door that separated the housemaster's private domain from the rest of the house.

The Quarrys never locked the baize door, which gave directly on to their sitting-room. They thought of their own rooms as an integral part of the house, and everyone, staff and pupils alike, respected their privacy. But now the door was opened tentatively, a head peered around, a voice called softly, 'Mrs Quarry?'

There was no answer, except for the noises from the kitchen. Up to this point the visitor had behaved perfectly naturally. No attempt had been made to enter the apartment unobserved. But, as the sounds continued and Mrs Quarry still didn't appear, a figure darted into the room, seized a bottle of gin from the drinks table, and made off with it. Helen Quarry continued with her cooking. She didn't hear the bottle smash against the banisters but, coming into the sitting-room a few minutes later, she heard a scream.

At once she dashed out of the apartment and along the corridor to the stairs. The first thing she noticed was a strong smell of gin. Then she saw the broken bottle and on the landing, a dozen steps down, a knot of girls and Paula Darby bending over someone. Quickly she picked her way down to them.

'What's happened? Who's been hurt?'

The group parted to let her see, and Paula Darby said, 'Betty slipped on the wet stair, but luckily she's not done much damage to herself.'

'Yes, I have, Miss Darby. I've bruised my shoulder and my ankle hurts. I think I've broken it. And look, I've cut my hand on the glass.'

'What were you doing with a bottle of gin anyway?' Helen Quarry demanded. She always did her best to be impartial but Betty Farrow, who was always inclined to make a fuss about nothing, was not a favourite. 'Well?' she added as

Betty, being helped to her feet by Paula Darby, didn't answer at once.

'It wasn't Betty, Mrs Quarry,' one of the other girls said. 'We were all together and we found this—this mess here. But of course it was Betty who slipped on it.' There was contempt in the young voice for the clumsy and unattractive.

'I see.'

'The secret drinker,' someone said.

It wasn't more than a whisper, but Helen caught the words. 'Who said that? What do you mean?'

The girls were giggling among themselves now and Paula Darby said sharply, 'Don't be stupid! Here, two of you help Betty along to matron. The rest of you get over to College House and find your next classes.'

The giggling stopped abruptly. The girls dispersed, Betty Farrow complaining to her reluctant helpers that she couldn't walk and they'd have to carry her. Paula Darby began to kick the broken bits of bottle against the wall.

'I'll get someone along to clear this up,' she said.

'Paula.' Helen Quarry was frowning. 'It was just a silly joke, wasn't it, that remark about a secret drinker? You seemed to react rather strongly.'

'Oh Lord!' Paula ran a hand through her pretty fair hair. 'You mean you've not heard the rumour that's going round the school?'

'What rumour?'

Paula Darby hesitated, looking at the older woman in some distress. 'About—about Sylvia Roystone—that she drinks too much, that she wasn't completely sober the night she had the accident.'

'But that's dreadful, and quite untrue.' Helen Quarry was appalled. 'How on earth could such a story have started? Hugh'll be furious when he gets to hear of it.'

'I know, but what can we do? What can he do, for that matter? He can hardly deny it! I suppose eventually it'll die away and be forgotten.'

'Well, at least we can clear up the mystery of this bottle of gin,' Helen said positively. 'And the sooner that's done the better. I'll get hold of John.'

Solving the mystery didn't prove as simple as Helen Quarry had anticipated. As soon as she returned to her sitting-room she saw that a bottle of gin was missing. But this fact, by itself, didn't help much.

'Any luck?' she said to her husband that evening.

'None. Blank-faced innocence all round. I don't like it, Helen. Somehow it doesn't strike me as just a prank.'

'Maybe we've got a secret drinker among the girls. That's the obvious explanation.'

'I find it hard to believe, though.' John Quarry shook his head. 'It'd be awfully difficult for one of them to conceal it, and I'm not sure the others would cover for her—not something like this. Of course it could be one of the domestic staff, or a teacher, or someone from another house or—'

'Not Sylvia Roystone?'

'No. She'd hardly need to pinch our gin, would she? Hugh can afford to buy her as much as she likes.'

Helen didn't smile. 'They'll be here soon. Are you going to tell them?'

'About the gin? Yes, though Hugh'll say it's a matter of house discipline, and leave it to me. But this rumour about Sylvia's a different matter. No and again no. We're not in the business of spreading rumours. We've not heard it. Let some other spirit, braver than I am, carry the bad news to him.'

'John!' Helen protested.

A knock on the door prevented her saying more. The Roystones had arrived—both of them, in spite of John Quarry's prediction. The evening passed pleasantly. Conversation was general: the weather, Helen's excellent cooking, the government's threat to make more changes in the examination system, the school's prospects in the various summer sports. Sylvia was quiet, but she seemed to be enjoying herself.

John Quarry saved the story of the stolen gin till they were having coffee. He was in the middle of it when the phone rang. Helen answered it.

'Hugh, it's for you. Sergeant Court from Colombury police station.'

Roystone took the receiver from her. 'Thanks.' He gave his name, listened briefly, said, 'Thanks,' again, and slowly replaced the receiver on the instrument. The others had stopped talking. He turned to face them.

'Bad news,' he said gruffly. 'Little Billy Morton died an hour ago and there'll have to be an inquest.'

CHAPTER 5

'. . . entrance is dependent, as you know, on his examination results, but we have every reason to expect that Peter will do well in his A-levels. With all best wishes, etc., etc.'

Hugh Roystone stopped dictating. He pushed back his chair, stood up and walked over to the window. It was a beautiful day and he could feel the early morning sun warm on his face. Later it would be hot. He ran a finger round the inside of his collar, regretting the need for his dark suit and sombre tie. His thoughts were on his wife, his expression grim.

In the distance he heard the sound of choral voices. On the still air he could even distinguish the words. It was one of the hymns that everyone liked, and they were belting it out with enthusiasm:

'Who would true valour see,
Let him come hither . . .'

Coriston had no chapel, but each morning at Assembly in

the Great Hall a prayer was said and a hymn was sung before matters of significance were dealt with and routine notices disposed of. It was normal for the headmaster to officiate. Today was different. Today John Quarry was taking Assembly.

Behind him Frances Bell coughed, and Hugh Roystone turned round to his secretary. 'Sorry!' he grinned ruefully. 'What else is there?'

Frances shuffled her papers, giving the headmaster time to adjust his thoughts. 'There's a complaint from Mrs Avelon. Ralph forgot to bring his pills back to school this term, and why has no one noticed that he's not taking them? They were delivered yesterday evening by her chauffeur. I've given them to Lyn Joyner and all is well, but Mrs A. will expect an apology from you.'

'You write her one, Frances. I'll sign it later.' Roystone looked at his watch. He could no longer hear singing. Assembly must be nearly over. He said, 'We've heard no more about that stolen gin, have we?'

'No. No one's confessed.' Frances Bell kept her eyes lowered. She had no intention of telling Hugh Roystone of the wild rumours that were circulating among the staff and, doubtless, among the pupils too. She changed the subject quickly. 'There's nothing else that can't wait, but Paula Darby asked me to remind you about the reference you promised her.'

'I've not forgotten.'

'I can't imagine why she's suddenly decided to leave Coriston and go and teach in Australia. As you know, we've been pretty good friends since she came to the school, but I've always felt she's a very private person, and she's certainly never really confided in me.' Frances Bell sounded a little aggrieved.

Roystone shrugged off the problem quickly. 'She's been here some while. There's no prospect of a vacancy for a housemistress, and she has relations in Sydney—a brother, isn't it? Everyone's not as—as devoted to Coriston as you are, Frances.'

Frances Bell ignored the implied compliment. She merely said, 'As far as I'm concerned, I'm happy here. It suits me.'

'Good. We're thankful,' Roystone said. He looked at his watch again. 'I must go. I'm sure one's expected to be punctual at an inquest. Look up Paula's file, and write a rough draft for me, will you? As full of praise as you can make it.'

'Right.' Frances hesitated, then wished him luck.

'Thanks,' Roystone said. 'They say there really shouldn't be any problems, but you never can tell—' With a resigned gesture he went through into his private apartment.

Frances Bell collected her papers. The phone in her office had started to ring, and she hurried to answer it. A headmaster in Yorkshire wished to speak to Mr Roystone; it was, his secretary claimed, in connection with the application of a Mr Simon Ford for the post of a senior mathematics master in the following school year. Frances informed the speaker that Mr Roystone was not in the College; he would phone back on his return.

Another departure, she thought, but not to be regretted, like Paula Darby's, and no reason to ask why. Ford hadn't appreciated the reprimand about his work that Roystone had been forced to deliver earlier in the year. It had been well deserved, for though Ford was a fine scholar, a fine mathematician, he was incorrigibly lazy. He enjoyed working with the brighter pupils, and was good at making friends with them, but he wouldn't bother with the less gifted. On the whole he'd be no loss.

Busy with her thoughts, Frances returned to the headmaster's study and took the vase of tired flowers from his desk. At the beginning of term she had abandoned her practice of changing them, expecting Sylvia Roystone to take over the task. But when Sylvia made no effort to do so, and the headmaster was himself forced to throw wilted flowers into his wastebasket, she had resumed her daily duty. She still enjoyed the small chore, though it gave her less pleasure now than it had in the past.

'You see, Mr Roystone, there really were no problems,' the lawyer said. 'I hardly feel I've earned my fee.'

Roystone laughed, partly with relief. 'There might have been some difficulty,' he said. 'As it was, very satisfactory.'

'Yes, indeed. "Death by misadventure." No blame. What we expected.'

Sylvia abruptly interrupted the two men's mutual congratulations. 'Why did the Mortons have to bring their other boy with them?' she said suddenly. 'He should have been in school. Greg, he's called. I keep on thinking that Billy would have grown up to look like him if I—if he'd not been killed.' There were tears in her voice.

The lawyer opened his mouth, but saw Roystone's face and desisted. Instead he made hurried farewells, while Hugh put an arm round Sylvia's shoulders and led her from the building that housed the Oxford coroner's court. 'Darling,' he said gently, 'you know that nothing's going to bring Billy back, but now this is over I promise I'll go and see the Mortons, and if I can help them in any way, I will. I couldn't contact them before, while the thing was *sub judice*, but now it's possible.'

'Thank you.'

'Look, Sylvia dear, I realize it won't be easy to forget this thing. That'll take time. But it really is over, and you've got to make an effort not to brood. Please, darling, for my sake.'

'All right. I'll try, Hugh.'

'Fine. Then let's go. We'll give ourselves a good lunch on the way home. But first let's have a drink at the Randolph. It always reminds me of my irresponsible undergraduate days—when you were still a toddler, darling.'

'That sounds nice, if you don't have to get back to school.'

'Coriston can take care of itself for a while. After all, John

Quarry's there if any crisis arises. Let's forget the place for an hour or two.'

But almost immediately this hope was proved impossible. As soon as they entered the bar Roystone recognized Mrs Farrow, Betty's mother, sitting in a corner by herself. She had seen them, and it was too late to retreat. He introduced Sylvia, and left the two women together while he went to collect drinks.

'I'm waiting for my son,' Mrs Farrow said. 'David's reading history at Pembroke. He was at Coriston too, but of course that would be before your time, Mrs Roystone.' She eyed the headmaster's new wife with an interest she made no attempt to disguise, obviously noting the simple grey linen dress, the expensive handbag and matching shoes, the large diamond on Sylvia's left hand. Satisfied, she suddenly asked, 'Incidentally, how's Betty's ankle?'

'Betty's ankle?' Sylvia looked blank.

'Yes. Betty. Betty Farrow. My daughter. The girl who slipped on a broken gin bottle and fell down some stairs in her house. Surely you knew about it, Mrs Roystone?' she said reproachfully. 'It was a very strange accident.'

'Betty's fine, Mrs Farrow.' Roystone, returning with the drinks, had caught the tail-end of the conversation and attempted to repair the damage by answering for Sylvia. 'The doctor says it's a very slight strain. She'll have forgotten it in a few days.'

'That's good.' Mrs Farrow gave Roystone a warm smile. Then her expression changed. 'But have you discovered how a broken gin bottle came to be on the stairs?'

'Not yet, I'm afraid.'

'You must, you know.' Mrs Farrow leant forward earnestly, directing the full force of her gaze at Roystone and ignoring Sylvia. 'Nothing destroys a school's reputation so quickly these days as rumours about drinking and drugs among the children, or—or among those responsible for them. Only last night I was saying the same thing to Lord

Penmereth at a dinner party. He thoroughly agreed with me.'

'I'm sure everyone agrees with you, Mrs Farrow.' Roystone was bland. 'But I don't think you need worry about Coriston on either score.'

Mrs Farrow cast a meaningful glance at Sylvia's glass; eager to get away from the encounter, Sylvia had drunk its contents quickly. 'I'm glad to have your reassurance, Mr Roystone.' She looked at the clock behind the bar. 'Good heavens! I can't think what's happened to my son. Wretched boy! He was to have met me half an hour ago. I must go and phone. You'll have to excuse me . . .'

As soon as she was out of earshot Roystone said. 'Bloody woman! Now I suppose old Penmereth will be ringing me up.'

'Who's Penmereth?' Sylvia asked.

'Only the Chairman of Coriston's Board of Governors,' Hugh Roystone said. 'He's a nice enough chap, but a bit pompous. And I happen to know he'd have preferred to appoint John Quarry as head instead of me. He was voted down and I got the job, but I don't think he's ever quite forgiven me.'

'Drink, drugs and sex are only the modern equivalent of wine, women and song.' Tony Pierson was pontificating. 'Whereas our parents indulged in wine, women and song—'

'Not my parents,' Peter Grey said firmly. 'Wine, perhaps. In fact, a good deal of wine. But never women and song. They don't even like opera.'

'Don't be so damned literal, Peter,' Pierson languidly reproached his friend. 'What do you think of this grass we're smoking? I was assured it was all excellent quality, but it seems to me these joints vary.'

'I'll have to take your word for it. My experience is sadly limited. So it is with drink—and sex, too,' Peter Grey added sadly.

Pierson laughed. 'Cheer up. We've all but finished with this dump. A few more weeks, then the summer vac, and after that—Oxford. Dreaming spires, girls galore—grown-up ones, I mean, not like those about here—drifting down the Isis in a punt, Commem balls—'

'You've forgotten something,' Grey interrupted. 'There's A-levels first. This may be a delightful way to spend a summer afternoon, but it's not going to help us with those bloody exam papers.'

The two boys were sitting in a small field, their backs against a disused shed, their legs stretched out in front of them. They were within the bounds of Coriston, but in an isolated part of the grounds, beyond the vegetable garden. Strictly speaking, they had no business to be there, but as sixth-formers and house prefects no one would have objected to their choosing a solitary place for study—and books were spread around them. So far this afternoon, however, they'd not done much work, content to laze and chat—and smoke.

They had drifted on to one of their favourite themes—the supposed sexual habits of their headmaster and his so much younger wife—when Pierson stopped in mid-sentence. Pinching out his joint, he gestured to Grey to do the same. Hurriedly they pulled books towards them and pretended to read. There was silence, then a smothered cough.

Pierson put a finger to his lips. Quietly he laid aside the book he was holding and got to his feet. Keeping close to the wall, he stole around the corner of the shed.

'Got you!' he said.

There was a short scream and a voice protested, 'No, no, Pierson. Don't hurt me, please.'

Pierson returned, marching before him a small boy. 'Guess what I've found,' he said.

'A worm,' Grey suggested. 'Or is it a mole?' He frowned fiercely. 'No, I see. It's Ralph Avelon.'

Pierson released his captive. 'You're not meant to be in

this part of the grounds, young Avelon. You know that
perfectly well. What were you up to? And how long have you
been here?'

'I was excused games. Matron told me to go for a walk
instead, and I heard your voices.' Avelon sniffed. 'You've
been smoking,' he said. 'I can smell it.'

The two older boys exchanged glances. 'I think it really is
a mole,' Pierson said, 'straight out of a spy story. Young
Avelon, have you ever been told about the three wise
monkeys—see no evil, hear no evil, speak no evil? You'd
better be all three wise monkeys rolled into one. You've seen
nothing and heard nothing—and smelt nothing—and if you
dare mention to a soul—'

'I won't, Pierson. I swear.' Avelon's big brown eyes
regarded Pierson solemnly. 'I wouldn't do anything to get
you into trouble. You know that.'

'Okay. I'll trust you. Off you go, then.'

Tony Pierson aimed a half-hearted kick in the direction of
Avelon's departing backside as the small boy ran off,
obviously undismayed. Then he threw himself down on the
ground again, took his half-smoked joint from his blazer
pocket, relit it and tossed the matches to Grey.

'We'll finish these, and then that's our quota for the day,'
he said.

Grey yawned. 'That kid Avelon is becoming a damned
nuisance. It's okay for him to worship you from afar,
but when he takes to following you around it's a different
matter.'

'Don't you worry about him. He'll keep his mouth shut.'
Pierson stretched himself indolently.

They continued with their earlier conversation. Relaxed
by the cannabis and in the aftermath of the scare that Avelon
had given them, they were totally unprepared for a second
interruption. Leyton caught them red-handed.

Having a free period at the end of the afternoon, Steve
Leyton had also decided on a walk. It was chance that led

him through the vegetable garden and beyond. He was
wandering along, scarcely noticing his whereabouts, his
mind preoccupied. He liked Coriston, he liked the staff, he
liked his pupils, but he was far from sure he liked teaching.
The trouble was that the alternative seemed to be unemploy-
ment. He had fallen into his present provisional appointment, for which he was only half-qualified, because his
mother was related to one of the governors. If Roystone
decided he was unsuitable his problem would be solved, but
did he want it solved in that way?

He was as unprepared to see Pierson and Grey when he
came round the corner of the shed as they were to see him.
After a second's hesitation they got slowly to their feet.
Pierson dropped the butt of his cigarette to the ground and
made a desultory attempt to bury it with his heel. Grey
followed suit, with even less enthusiasm.

'Trying to get rid of the evidence?' Leyton asked
pleasantly.

'Not really, sir.' Pierson's grin was lop-sided. 'It wouldn't
be much use, would it?'

'None.' Leyton let the monosyllable hang. Then he added,
'A fair cop, wouldn't you say?'

There was another pause before Pierson said, 'I suppose
you couldn't forget about this, sir?' He tried to sound hope-
ful. 'It's just an experiment, really it is. We don't make a
habit of it. Only a couple of times in the holidays and a little
this term.'

'Where did you get it from?'

'A friend of mine—no one connected with the school—
gave it to me at Easter,' Pierson said.

'And you shared it with Grey, of course. Anyone else?'

'No, sir.'

'Okay. How much was there? How much have you left?'

Reluctantly Pierson produced from his blazer pocket a
rather battered tin box. He handed it to Leyton. Inside were
six dark brown cigarettes, obviously hand-rolled and with

twisted ends; the box might originally have contained about twenty.

'And that's all you've got now? Anywhere?'

'Yes, sir. As I said, we don't make a habit of it.'

'Please, Mr Leyton, can't you forget it?' Peter Grey added his plea. 'If you tell the head he'll be livid and he'll tell our parents. Heaven knows how my father'll react. He's terribly down on drugs and all that sort of thing.'

Steve Leyton hesitated. He knew the school rules. He knew he should report the two of them to the headmaster. But they weren't children; in a few weeks they'd be at university, and what they did would be of no further concern to the school. Besides, it hadn't been long since he'd been experimenting with the stuff himself. It had done him no harm. Perhaps it was stupid to create an unnecessary fuss over something that probably wasn't really serious. He made up his mind.

'All right. Give me your word, both of you—no more cannabis or anything else in that line till you're free of Coriston—and I'll pretend we never met this afternoon. Is that a bargain?'

'Yes, sir. Thank you.'

'Thank you, sir.'

'Don't mention it.' In spite of himself Leyton found himself grinning at them. 'Just make sure you've got that unmistakable hemp smell out of your hair and clothes before you go back to your house, or Mr Joyner's going to guess anyway.'

CHAPTER 6

The following Saturday the traditional cricket match between staff and pupils took place at Coriston. Occasionally in recent years a mistress or one or two of the girls had found places in the teams, but usually the players were confined to

masters and boys. It was one of the school's conceits that the
day was always fine, and this particular Saturday was no
exception. The sky was blue with a scattering of fluffy white
cloud. The temperature was pushing the mid-seventies. A
slight breeze ruffled the hair of the out-fielders and refreshed
the spectators sitting in deck-chairs in front of the pavilion
or lying casually on the grass around the boundary.

The boys won the toss, batted first and made a hundred
and eighty-five runs. Of these Tony Pierson contributed half
a century. On the master's side, Steve Leyton had brought
off a spectacular catch and the headmaster, a slow bowler,
had taken two wickets; no one, in either team, had disgraced
himself.

The staff now had high hopes. The opposition was weaker
than in some previous years, and their own team's strength
had been enhanced by the presence of Leyton, who was an
Oxford 'blue'. He was clearly a considerable acquisition, and
they were counting on him for a good score. Mark Joyner,
who was steady and reliable, had opened the batting with
John Quarry, and between them they had so far made fifteen
runs.

'John's brilliant but erratic,' his wife said as Quarry made
four runs from the first ball of the next over, and completely
missed the second.

'That's because he doesn't really take the match
seriously,' Hugh Roystone complained.

'Should he?' Sylvia asked idly. 'Is it so serious?' She knew
little or nothing about cricket, except that the game bored
her, but Hugh had insisted she should come and watch.

'Of course it's serious,' Roystone said sharply. 'There'd be
no point in it otherwise, would there?'

A sudden groan from Lyn Joyner, who was sitting with
them, relieved Sylvia of the need to answer the unanswer-
able. 'Mark's gone!' she exclaimed. 'Clean bowled. Oh dear,
he will be upset.'

Hugh Roystone, already padded up, got to his feet and

picked up his bat. There were various cries of 'Good luck, sir'
and 'Good luck, headmaster' as he made his way to the
wicket. Joyner passed him, looking as disconsolate as his wife
had predicted, to be greeted with polite clapping from the
spectators by the pavilion.

Further along the row of chairs, Simon Ford, cleaning his
spectacles, began to take more interest in the game. 'If only
our revered head could be out first ball,' he said, 'I'd
willingly give a fiver to the boy who brought it about.'

Paula Darby laughed, but Steve Leyton reacted quickly.
'Don't say that. I'm in next, and I need time to get used to the
idea. I'm horribly nervous. I'm sure I'll make a mess of
things.'

'Nonsense,' Paula said. 'You'll do fine, Steve.'

'Aim at young Grey over there,' Ford said. 'He looks half
asleep to me, absolutely doped. He'll let anything go by.'

Leyton sat up abruptly. 'What? Oh no! He can't be.
Doped, I mean.' He stared in the direction of Peter Grey.
'You must be wrong. They promised—'

'Steve, Simon wasn't suggesting that Grey was literally
drugged,' Paula said gently.

Ford was grinning. 'Wasn't I?' he said. 'And what did
"they"—presumably Grey and Pierson—promise you,
Steve? Come on, tell us.'

'I can't.'

'Shall I guess? You caught them—smoking pot, perhaps—
and they promised never again.'

Leyton nodded miserably. 'Okay. That's right.'

'And you didn't report them? Steve, it's considered a
serious offence here at Coriston,' Paula protested.

'I know, but—' Leyton explained briefly, ignoring the
intermittent clapping as John Quarry continued to add to his
score. 'Anyway, I made a bargain with them. I can't turn
them in now.'

'Not without turning yourself in too,' said Ford. 'And
what's done is done. Okay, I won't tell, if Paula agrees.'

'Well, for your sake, Steve—all right,' Paula said.

'Thanks, both of you.' Leyton was relieved. He turned his attention to the cricket. 'Ah, the head's got the strike at last,' he said.

They watched as the school captain delivered the first ball of the new over. It was fast, and it skidded on a dent in the pitch. Roystone was lucky to get his bat to it. It flew behind him at an angle, and he was not immediately sure of where it had gone.

'Run!' Quarry shouted as Roystone hesitated.

Roystone ran. But he'd covered no more than two yards when he heard the snick of the bails behind him, and a cry of 'How's that?' He turned, disbelieving what he saw. His wicket was done. He was out for a duck—run out by Quarry's stupid call.

'My dear chap—headmaster—I am sorry.' Quarry came loping up to him.

'Couldn't you have seen—' Roystone began, and stopped himself; there was no point in giving Quarry the satisfaction of knowing he was angry. He managed to smile. 'Better not run out Steve Leyton,' he said.

'Oh, I won't do that,' Quarry said. 'I wouldn't dream of it.'

Hugh Roystone was already striding off the field, his bat under his arm, and he didn't hear Quarry's last remark. Passing Leyton on his way he wished him luck. With two wickets down, the staff certainly needed it.

Aware of his Oxford reputation and a little shaken by the headmaster's ill fortune, Leyton was nervous. He played himself in carefully. Then there was a short ball, a gift to any batsman, and he hit it with all his strength. But something went wrong. Instead of soaring to the boundary the ball flew high in the air and fell as a catch a child could have taken. Somehow Tony Pierson let it slip through his fingers.

Later, after the masters had won the match by two wickets, mainly due to Leyton's innings, Pierson excused himself on the grounds that the sun had been in his eyes. Only to Peter Grey did he add, 'I felt we owed Steve Leyton, and what's a game of cricket, after all?' It wasn't an attitude of which his headmaster would have approved.

There were other conversations that evening critical of the players. If anything, Helen Quarry shared Pierson's view of the importance of the match, but she was annoyed with her husband.

'You did it on purpose, John. You know you did, and Hugh knows it too. It was so obvious. Why?'

'Why, my dear? I just did it to annoy. I couldn't resist the chance to run him out. I get a little tired of the great man sometimes. And he's been on about that damned bottle of gin again. You might think we set it up on the stairs as a booby-trap for the Farrow girl.'

'I gather Mrs Farrow's been complaining. And Lord Penmereth.'

'So what? It's part of Roystone's job to deal with them,' Quarry said irritably.

There was a rap on the door, and the school secretary put her head around the green baize. 'May I come in?'

'Yes, come along,' Helen said. 'I've just put the coffee on, but John says we need something stronger first.'

'Excellent idea. I certainly do.' With a sigh Frances Bell collapsed into an armchair. 'It's been a nerve-racking week. Thank goodness that damned inquest's over.'

'And very satisfactorily,' Helen said.

'Not from the Mortons' point of view.' Quarry was busy pouring drinks. 'With that verdict they've not much chance of a successful claim. So they've lost their child, with no compensation.'

'But it's right that Sylvia should have been cleared of blame,' Helen protested. 'I only hope these wretched rumours about her drinking will die down now.'

Frances agreed, and the conversation turned to other

topics—the Quarrys' two sons at Cambridge, their married daughter, school gossip and the coming half-term break.

'You're going away?' Frances asked.

'No, not this time.' Helen was quick to explain. 'All the senior staff can't go at once, and we thought it only fair to let Hugh and Sylvia have a few days off. They never had a proper honeymoon, and this term, with the accident and everything, must have been an awful strain for both of them—especially for Sylvia. Hugh's got his work, but now she refuses to drive a car any more she gets no relief from this place. It's hard for her even to get into Oxford for an hour or two.'

'Yes. Poor dears!" Quarry said with an undertone of sarcasm.

The two women exchanged quick glances of understanding, and Frances said brightly, 'Well, they certainly didn't spend last Easter gallivanting round North America like you two.'

'Gallivanting!' John Quarry laughed.

And Frances, sensing that she'd somehow said the wrong thing, changed the subject. 'I'm spending half-term at Fairfield, at Paula Darby's cottage.' She hesitated. 'As a matter of fact, I'm considering buying it when she goes to Australia.'

'I see,' said Helen. 'We wondered what she'd be doing with the place.'

'Would you be interested? I'm not sure how much she's asking, though it'll probably be more than I can afford. But it's a nice little house.'

'It may be a nice house, but it's not very useful, Frances,' Quarry said. 'It's too far from here for daily commuting. Like Paula, you could only use it for half-terms and holidays and the occasional weekend. And there's the upkeep to worry about.'

'I realize all that, John. But I was thinking that if I bought it now I'd have somewhere to go when I retire. It's looking

ahead, of course, but by the time I've paid off a mortgage—'
She was interrupted by the sound of feet pounding down the
corridor, and a heavy knocking at the door. 'What on earth?'

John Quarry leapt from his chair and pulled the door
open. 'What is it?' he demanded.

'Come quickly, Mr Quarry, please. It's Jane—Jane
Hilman.' Betty Farrow was gasping for breath. 'We think
she's drowned. She's been in a bathroom for ages, and she
doesn't answer. We don't know what to do.'

Quarry asked no questions. He ran, followed by the two
women and the girl. They found a cluster of girls, most of
them in their dressing-gowns ready for bed, standing in a
corridor outside one of the bathrooms. As Quarry came up
two of the house prefects were hurling themselves at the door.
It shook, but didn't give.

'Here, let me,' Quarry ordered at once.

Either because the bolt had been weakened, or because
John Quarry was heavier, the door burst open at his first
onslaught. He staggered into the hot, steaming room. Jane
Hilman, a pretty sixteen-year-old, was lying in the bath, her
long fair hair floating round her, her eyes closed. But by some
miracle she hadn't slipped completely under the water; her
nose and mouth were above the surface, and her breasts
were rising and falling. There was no doubt she was still
breathing.

Quarry, with Helen's help, lifted her from the bath and
wrapped her in a large towel. He carried her to the bed-study
room she shared with Betty Farrow. Frances Bell dispersed
the group of anxious girls, assuring them that Jane would be
all right, and told the prefects to fetch Mrs Cole, the matron,
who was a qualified nurse.

Waiting, Helen and Frances stood looking down at Jane,
uncertain what action to take. Quarry hovered in the doorway with Betty Farrow.

'Shall I send for the doctor?' Quarry asked. 'What do you
think?'

'No—no, please. I don't need a doctor.' Jane Hilman's eyes had fluttered open, and she answered for herself. 'I'm all right. Really. I must—must have fainted. I expect the water was too hot.'

'We'll see what Mrs Cole says.' Helen was firm. 'She'll be here in a minute. Just lie quiet, Jane.'

'I'm sorry Mrs Quarry—everyone. I didn't mean to cause a fuss and upset you all.'

'My dear, don't worry about us,' Helen Quarry said. 'We're just thankful you've come to no harm.'

'You might have been drowned—dead—if I hadn't gone to look for you,' Betty Farrow said suddenly. 'I saved your life.'

'Thank you. I'm very grateful, Betty.' Jane spoke with little conviction, but she managed a weak smile.

'Dead,' Betty Farrow repeated, and it was she who began to cry.

CHAPTER 7

The Roystones took advantage of the long half-term break and went to Paris. It was a successful trip, which they both enjoyed. It really looked to Hugh as if Sylvia was beginning to put the accident behind her, and they both returned to Coriston happier than they had been at any time since Billy Morton died.

The second half of Trinity Term was always busy. There were of course the public examinations, together with a full schedule of sporting events and, to crown everything, Founder's Day, when the governors paid their annual formal visit and the school was *en fête*, open to parents and prospective parents alike. In many ways it was Hugh Roystone's favourite period. This year, because he hoped that it might serve further to distract his wife, he looked forward to it even more than usual.

It was on the third day after the half-term break that the headmaster, on his way to his normally private pre-breakfast swim, hurried through the main doors of the building that housed the swimming pool. He was surprised and not a little annoyed to hear female voices. He was slightly later than usual, but he still couldn't imagine who would be there ahead of him. He peered through the glass half of the swing doors that led to the pool itself to see Margaret Seymour, one of the physical education teachers, in the water with Betty Farrow.

Shrugging his shoulders, he turned right to the boys' changing rooms, undressed quickly and returned. Margaret Seymour and Betty looked up as he came in.

'Good morning,' he said cheerfully, sitting on the edge of the pool and dangling his feet in the water.

'Good morning, headmaster. I—I'm so sorry we're still here,' Margaret Seymour apologized, for Hugh Roystone's predilection for lone early morning exercise was well known. 'I hoped we'd be finished long ago, but we don't seem to make any progress.' She cast a resigned glance at Betty in her regulation swimsuit. Betty's mouth, Roystone saw, was set in an obstinate line.

Betty seized her opportunity. 'Can I go then, Miss Seymour? We mustn't disturb Mr Roystone.' She began to swim to the steps at the side of the pool, keeping her head well out of the water.

'You're not disturbing me, Betty,' Roystone said at once. He looked inquiringly at the PE mistress. 'What's the problem?'

'It's silly, headmaster. Betty's quite a good little swimmer, but she won't put her head under. She could be in the school team if only—' Margaret Seymour contained her exasperation. 'I thought perhaps if I brought her here early when no one else was about—'

'Yes, of course.' Roystone was quick to understand. 'Can't

I help? Come on, Betty. Miss Seymour and I will stand either side of you and help you do a duck dive. Once you've done one or two you'll see how easy it is and you won't mind any more.'

Betty Farrow turned back and swam slowly towards the headmaster. Coming from him, it was more than a mere request. It was an order, and she couldn't refuse. But her face showed her resentment.

And Roystone had underestimated the girl's fear. To him it seemed the simplest thing in the world to flip her over in the water. He wasn't expecting her to resist, to try to seize on to him, to struggle violently. His hand slipped up between her legs, and instinctively she kicked him as he released her.

With Miss Seymour's help, Betty came up, choking and spluttering. Roystone was laughing; the kick hadn't been hard. 'My dear Betty, I'm sorry. Shall we have another go?'

'No! No! It was horrid!'

'I think perhaps, headmaster—' Margaret Seymour began tactfully.

'Yes, I'm sure you're right. Okay. Enough for today, Betty.' Roystone agreed and, in an effort to be affable, added, 'Incidentally, how's Jane, your room-mate? Not been fainting again, I hope.'

'I don't know how she is, Mr Roystone. We're not friends any more. She blames me for the rumour going round that she tried to drown herself that day in the bath, and it wasn't me that started it—it really wasn't.' By now Betty had recovered from her ducking, and was aggrieved. 'Can I go and change, please? I'm cold.'

'Of course. Off you go. Have a warm shower.'

Roystone exchanged glances with Margaret Seymour as she followed the girl from the pool. He was disturbed by Betty Farrow's comments, but this clearly wasn't the time or the place to discuss the matter. He put it out of his mind for the moment, and concentrated on his morning swim.

However, later in the day Roystone met John Quarry in

College House and invited him and Helen to drop in after supper. 'One or two things—house matters—I'd like to discuss,' he said, and left Quarry to wonder.

'You don't think he's going to mention that damned bottle of gin again, do you?' Quarry said to Helen as they strolled through the warm summer evening towards the headmaster's apartment. 'What else is there? Apart from the usual exam fever, everything's going pretty smoothly.'

Helen frowned. For once her usually equable temperament was disturbed. She'd had a slight headache since she got out of bed that morning, and was feeling decidedly out of sorts. She would have much preferred bed to the Roystones', but she knew that the headmaster often used a casual invitation as an excuse to discuss something that was troubling him.

That evening he came quickly to the point. He described his attempt to teach Betty Farrow to duck dive, making it an amusing anecdote. Then, suddenly serious, he inquired if they thought Jane Hilman was unhappy.

It was Helen who answered. 'Yes,' she said. 'I think she is—fairly so, anyway. She says she's afraid her parents won't let her come back here next term. They think O-levels are enough for her, it seems.'

'But that's ridiculous!' Roystone was indignant. 'What on earth do they propose to do with the poor girl?' He turned to Sylvia, to explain. 'The Hilmans live in the depths of Gloucestershire, miles from anywhere. The father's some kind of recluse. They never leave the place, and only occasionally have a relative to stay. It would be a ghastly life for a young girl.'

'How did they come to send her here in the first place?' Sylvia asked.

'A cousin who knew one of our governors finally persuaded them,' Quarry said. 'Jane had been educated at home before, and I gather the local education authority wasn't satisfied and said she must go to school. None of us have ever met the

parents. They never come to any of the Coriston affairs, but
Hugh and I have both corresponded with them and they
sound dreadful. Victorian's not the word for them; they seem
so old-fashioned as to be almost unbelievable. I've sometimes wondered if they realize Coriston's coeducational.'

'And Jane's a nice child,' Helen said.

'And bright,' Quarry added.

'She is indeed, especially at maths. She seems to have
taken to these new computers like a duck to water.' Roystone
paused. 'Not a very appropriate simile,' he added. 'I was
horrified when Betty Farrow let slip this rumour that Jane
was trying to drown herself in the bath that day earlier in the
term.'

'It's just another damned rumour,' Helen said angrily.
'There's no more truth in it than the one about—' She
stopped short, suddenly aware of what she had been about to
say.

'One about what?' Roystone said. 'Don't tell me there are
more rumours flying around that I haven't heard.'

'No, no. I'm sorry,' Helen said quickly. 'I wasn't really
thinking clearly. I've a bit of a headache.'

'You've got to expect a fair crop of rumours in a place like
this. It'd be the same in any enclosed society. I bet a
nunnery's a hotbed.' Quarry tried to distract attention from
his wife's confusion.

Sylvia came to their rescue. 'Please,' she said unexpectedly. 'I can perfectly well guess what Helen was about to
say.' She looked at the Quarrys, and then at her husband.
Her colour had risen. 'A few days ago I was sitting in our
garden, reading, and I heard a couple of the boys talking on
the other side of the wall. I don't know who they were, but
they were speaking of me. They said I was lucky the inquest
hadn't asked about my—my drinking habits—only they
didn't put it quite like that. And—and they mentioned my
drinking quite casually, as if it were generally accepted I was
a kind of alcoholic.'

Hugh Roystone had been listening with growing anger. Now he exploded. 'When was this?' he demanded of his wife. 'Why in God's name didn't you tell me before?' And of Quarry, 'Did you know? Why wasn't I told? It's disgraceful that this sort of thing should go on without my knowing. We must do something about it at once.'

'But what?' said Quarry. 'That's the point, Hugh. Denials—inquiries—all that sort of thing would only make matters worse, and make Jane—and Sylvia—look silly. The only answer's something an American once suggested for a different kind of problem—"benign neglect".'

This was not a solution that Hugh Roystone found easy to accept. But he had little time to brood over it, for the next day he was faced with a problem more serious and immediate than how to scotch unpleasant rumours. Little Ralph Avelon disappeared.

Mrs Avelon, before her marriage, had aspired to the opera stage. Her professionally trained voice was still beautiful and, given a little encouragement, she would sing for her friends. She was determined that Ralph should grow up to appreciate music, even though he might never be a practising musician, and had arranged for him to have extra tuition at Coriston. It was unfortunate—and, to Mrs Avelon, irrelevant—that, like his father, Ralph was tone deaf and hated the music lessons which kept him from more interesting pursuits. Mrs Avelon was resolute.

So, in his way, was Ralph. He took every opportunity to dodge the lessons he detested and when, for the umpteenth time, he failed to turn up, the music master merely sighed with relief and read a book until the period was over.

Ralph wasn't missed until prep. Even then someone suggested that he had gone to see matron and his absence was accepted. It was not until after supper that any concern began to be shown, and still there was no great alarm. But Simon Ford, who happened to be on duty that evening, made some inquiries. By nine o'clock, when Ralph hadn't re-appeared, Ford reported the matter to Mark Joyner, the boy's housemaster.

'What do you mean, young Avelon's missing?'

'Just what I say.' Ford took off his spectacles and polished the lenses on his handkerchief. 'No one's seen him since lunch. He cut his music lesson and—'

'Why the hell didn't you tell me before?'

'For the simple reason I only recently became aware of it myself.' Ford replaced his spectacles. 'And before I pushed the panic button I thought it wise to make sure he wasn't lurking in the infirmary or some such place. Do you suppose he's run off home?'

'I've no idea. Nor am I going to waste more time wonder-ing.' Joyner spoke tartly. 'I'll inform the head and I imagine he'll order a search of the buildings and grounds before we take any more drastic action.'

Roystone acted quickly. All available staff and a few of the more senior prefects were organized into pairs, and each pair allocated a given area. The headmaster knew that if nothing came of the search he would have to phone Mrs Avelon and notify the police. It could probably be said that he'd delayed too long already.

It was a great pity the wretched child hadn't been missed sooner, the headmaster ruminated as he paced up and down his sitting-room. Possibly old-fashioned schools with call-overs at a set hour every day had their advantage. He turned to the window and stared out as dusk gave way to darkness. Sylvia sat and stared at a book. There was nothing either of them could do but wait for news. When—if—Ralph Avelon was found he was to be taken straight to the infirmary, and Mrs Cole had alerted the school doctor.

Each time the phone rang Roystone leapt to answer it, but again and again the news was negative. In fact, it was over an hour before Ralph Avelon was found, in a shed on the edge of the vegetable garden—the same shed that had supported the backs of Pierson and Grey two or three weeks ago as they smoked their cannabis.

In the small enclosed space of the shed the same hemp-like smell was overpowering, and Mark Joyner wrinkled his nose in disgust as he swung his torch around. 'Christ!' he said under his breath as the beam of light picked out first a pool of vomit, then the body of Ralph Avelon stretched full length on the ground, his head under one of the potting shelves.

'Here, hold this.' He handed the torch to Peter Grey, who was with him, and dropped to his knees beside Avelon. 'He's dead to the world,' he said.

'Dead? Oh no! It couldn't kill him.' Grey's voice was high with shock.

'Don't be a fool, Grey.' Joyner was harsh. 'He's alive all right, thank God. He's passed out, unconscious. For heaven's sake, what's the matter with you? Keep the light steady!'

'I'm sorry, sir.'

The swinging beam had momentarily moved sideways, and in its light could be glimpsed a partly-smoked dark-brown roll, lying by Avelon's outstretched hand. Redirecting the light as his housemaster had ordered, Grey bent down. He was reaching out towards the cigarette when Joyner said sharply, 'What's that? Have you found one of the joints the little idiot's been smoking?'

'I—I think so, sir.'

'Good. Put it in your pocket. Then help me lift him over my shoulder. That'll be the best way to carry him. Lucky he's small.'

'Let me carry him, sir. Please.'

Joyner glanced at Grey. At eighteen Peter Grey was almost a head taller and several inches broader than the housemaster. The suggestion was perfectly reasonable, but there had been a curious urgency about it, and since they'd found Avelon the older boy had been oddly nervous. Mark

Joyner dismissed his wandering thoughts.

'Okay,' he said. 'But let's hurry. The sooner we get him to the infirmary and tell the headmaster the better.'

CHAPTER 8

The following day would be long remembered at Coriston. For the second time that term John Quarry took Assembly and, before dismissing the school, he said, 'I have an important announcement to make. Please listen carefully.'

A shiver seemed to pass among the assembled pupils in the hall, like a sudden breath of wind across a cornfield. Feet shuffled, chairs creaked, one or two coughs were suppressed. On the platform, behind the deputy head, members of the staff suddenly fidgeted. Then everything was still. There were few who hadn't heard about Ralph Avelon, though the stories varied and were often far from accurate. No one had any difficulty in guessing at what was to come.

Quarry didn't disappoint them. 'Yesterday, as you probably know, Ralph Avelon was missing.' He paused and surveyed the young, upturned faces in front of him. 'He was found in a garden shed, unconscious. He had been smoking cannabis, possibly adulterated or combined with some other dangerous drug. He is a very sick boy. So listen to me. If any one of you knows or suspects where Avelon acquired this—this drug, if any one of you knows or suspects where there might be more of it in the school—or outside for that matter—you are to report what you know or suspect to your housemaster or your housemistress immediately. Immediately, I say. If any of you can help in any way, it is your duty to come forward. Forget your juvenile codes of conduct. This is a very serious matter indeed—it could well be a criminal matter—and it affects the good name of the school and of everyone here. If you know anything, consult your

housemaster or mistress at once. It will be better for all of us in the end.'

Quarry paused again. A tall figure, imposing in his long black gown, he purposely let the silence lengthen, giving everyone present, boys, girls and staff, time to become uncomfortable. Then he said, 'The headmaster wishes me to add that he expects to have a full explanation of this affair by the end of the day. He regrets that he is unable to be here this morning to impress on you himself the importance of the matter, but he is even now awaiting the arrival of Ralph Avelon's mother.'

It was exactly the right note on which to end Assembly.

The school dismissed, with but one topic of conversation. For most it was an exciting, though impressive, tidbit for gossip and speculation. For some, remembering their activities during the half-term break, it was a cause of anxiety, however peripheral. For a few, it posed a crisis—of conscience and alarm.

'What the hell are we going to do?' Peter Grey demanded as he and Pierson went off together to a maths lesson.

'Nothing.'

'Nothing? Tony, this is for real! We're in trouble, up to our necks.'

'We must play it cool, Peter. Act as if we're not involved. After all, it's nothing to do with us.'

'But we are and it is!' Grey was sweating. 'It's obvious what happened. Avelon caught us smoking. You're his great hero, so he decided to copy us. He must have got hold of the stuff in the half-term break—poor quality, mixed with God knows what—and brought it back with him.' He stopped suddenly and stared at Pierson. 'Unless you had some more and—'

'Don't worry about that, Peter. I gave nothing to Avelon. And neither of us can be blamed for what he might or might not have done in the break.'

'Can't we just? You try telling that to Roystone—or Joyner. What about prefects setting good examples and all that rot? You don't imagine Leyton's not going to shop us now, do you? It was decent of him to keep quiet before, but we can't expect—'

'Shut up! Talk of the devil—'

Steve Leyton was striding down the corridor towards them, his usually cheerful expression clouded. He had taken part in the search the previous evening, but there had not been time before Assembly to inform all the staff of the circumstances in which the boy had eventually been found. John Quarry's announcement had come as a complete surprise to him, and not a pleasant one.

Now, preoccupied, head down, brows creased, wrestling with his problem, Leyton might have passed Pierson and Grey without noticing them, but Pierson said loudly, 'Good morning, sir.'

Leyton stopped and raised his head abruptly. 'Is that really what you think?' he said.

Pierson made no attempt to misunderstand. 'Sir,' he said, 'it's nothing to do with us. We can't help. We don't know where Avelon got his stuff.'

'You're sure of that?' said Leyton sharply. 'I'm already in a totally invidious position because of you two, and if you've anything—anything whatsoever—to do with this, I swear I'll do my best to see that the head throws the book at you. In court as well as here at Coriston. Peddling drugs is a criminal matter, as Mr Quarry said.'

Tony Pierson's gaze was level. 'We most certainly didn't give any drugs to Avelon, sir, let alone sell him any. We didn't have any to give. You took all our joints and that was that, as far as we were concerned. We've kept our promise to you. Are you going to tell the head?'

In the face of this direct question Leyton hesitated. 'I don't know. I accept what you say—that yours was a separate incident—but I'm not sure the head would agree with me.

I'm not sure he should. In his position I'd want all the facts, directly relevant or not.'

'Sir,' Grey said. 'Can't Avelon say where he got his stuff?'

'When he's well enough to be questioned, doubtless he will, but—' Steve Leyton looked at his watch. 'I can't discuss it any more right now. I'm already late for my class. I'll see you in your study at six this evening. Maybe by then you'll be in the clear.'

'Let's hope so,' Pierson said as Leyton hurried off. He grinned at Grey, but his grin was forced.

Paula Darby had a free period first thing that morning; the class she should have been taking was writing an exam, and as it was on one of the subjects she taught she couldn't be asked to invigilate. But she had attended Assembly, and had managed to speak to Simon Ford immediately afterwards.

The conversation had been unsatisfactory. Ford had said, 'My dear, I was watching the cricket match. I remember Steve Leyton waffling to us at one point, but I can't remember a word he said. The game was too exciting. It had my full attention. And if you've any sense, Paula, it had your full attention too.'

'But Roystone must be told. If we've got a drug problem in the school, it's only fair to him—'

'Who's talking about fairness? If you must meddle, Paula, it's nothing to do with me. And please don't mention my name. I don't want to be connected with the matter. And there's absolutely no reason why I should be.'

Ford had turned and left her. Annoyed by his attitude, Paula had gone in search of Steve Leyton, but when she found him she could see through the glass-panelled door that he was already teaching. She resigned herself to waiting and went along to one of the staff rooms, where cups of coffee were usually available. At this time—the first period after Assembly—the room was empty; ordinary free periods were usually scheduled for later in the day. Paula was restless. She made a half-hearted attempt to look at a magazine. She glanced through her notes for her next class. She wandered over to a window which overlooked the entrance to College House. And she witnessed the arrival of Mrs Avelon.

The silver-grey Rolls drew up smoothly, the merest whisper of gravel beneath its wheels. The uniformed chauffeur leapt from his seat and opened the door for Mrs Avelon to emerge. This she did slowly—she had put on a little weight in the last few months— and purposefully. She was wearing a simple expensive white dress, a red straw hat and red accessories. She looked as if she were about to attend a garden fête or, more probably, open one in aid of a well-known charity.

A man descended after her. For a moment Paula wondered if he were Mr Avelon, dragged by the crisis from his business affairs, which in the past had always been too pressing to permit him to visit Coriston. Then she saw the unmistakable black bag. Mrs Avelon had brought her own doctor. Paula felt sorry for Hugh Roystone.

The sight of Mrs Avelon had made up Paula Darby's mind for her. A minute or two later she left the staff room and went along to Frances Bell's office. The door to the headmaster's study was not properly closed, and as she came into the outer room Paula could hear Mrs Avelon's resonant—almost operatic—voice.

'No, Mr Roystone, you listen to me! I gave my Ralph into your care. I entrusted him to you. I paid you handsomely to educate him, and to ensure that no harm came to him. You have heard the phrase *in loco parentis*, I'm sure. But you have abused my trust. You have let my boy be corrupted. And corrupted by drugs. Drugs!'

'Mrs Avelon, that's not true. Ralph—'

Mrs Avelon swept the protest aside. Sitting at her desk, unashamedly listening, Frances Bell made a face at Paula Darby. Paula grinned in sympathy, and together they waited while Mrs Avelon continued with her tirade.

'. . . propose to inform the governors that Coriston is no
longer a reputable school, a safe haven for young children.
But first of all I intend to remove my Ralph. I've brought my
own doctor with me, and if you'll show me the way to your
infirmary—and Dr Robertson says that it's not dangerous to
move him—I shall relieve you of my son's care. A care, I may
add, to which you seem to have paid little attention.'

'Very well, Mrs Avelon. If that's what you wish.' Roystone
had controlled his rising temper. 'Please come with me.'

Roystone opened the door of his study and led Mrs
Avelon, followed by the silent doctor, through the office. He
looked blankly at Paula, and said, 'Frances, please phone
Mrs Cole, and tell her to expect Mrs Avelon and myself
and—er—Dr Robertson.'

'Yes, headmaster,' Frances said, and 'Phew!' she added as
the door of the office closed behind the door. She reached for
the telephone. 'Poor Hugh!'

'Do you think she's really going to complain to the
governors?' Paula asked. 'What will they do?'

Frances shook her head. The phone in the infirmary had
been answered. 'Hello, Mrs Cole,' she said. 'Visitors for
you.' Quickly she explained, and smiled at the matron's
uncomplimentary comment.

Then she turned back to Paula. 'And what can I do for
you? Not some other calamity, I hope.'

'It's the same one, Frances, I'm afraid. Look, shortly
before half-term Steve Leyton caught Pierson and Grey
smoking pot. He let them off with a caution and didn't report
it, which was damned stupid of him. By the time I heard
about it, I couldn't do anything without getting poor Steve
into trouble, so I let it go. I know I shouldn't have, but I did.'
Paula shrugged defensively. 'Things are a bit different now,
though.'

'Could the two incidents be connected?'

'I don't see why not. Little Avelon's one of Pierson's
greatest fans. But I don't know any more for sure.' Paula

glanced up at the clock on the wall. 'Frances, I've a class. I'll
have to go. I know it's a lot to ask, but will you pass on what
I've said—with my sincere apologies. I feel awfully bad
about it.'

'Yes, of course I will. And don't worry. The head'll
understand.' Frances smiled as Paula left, but she added to
herself, 'I hope.'

At that moment Hugh Roystone was not in the most understanding of moods. Flanked by an irate Mrs Cole, he had
watched Dr Robertson lift the blanket-wrapped form of
Ralph Avelon into the back of the Rolls so that the boy's head
rested on his mother's lap. Then, with a nervous grimace, the
doctor had got into the front, the chauffeur had shut the
doors, the car had glided away, metaphorically scraping
Coriston's gravel off its tyres for ever. Mrs Avelon had not
acknowledged Roystone's farewells.

'What a rude woman!' the matron said.

'I'm sorry she was offensive to you.'

'I'm not troubled about myself, headmaster, but for her to
speak like that to you—why, it's disgraceful!' Mrs Cole had
no hesitation in speaking her mind. 'I defy anyone to say the
children could be better looked after than they are here.'

Roystone hoped the governors would agree. He doubted
it. Coriston depended to a great extent on its reputation for
individual care of its pupils, and the sudden removal of
Ralph Avelon in such unhappy circumstances could do
nothing but harm to that reputation. At the very least Mrs
Avelon would be sure to spread the news among her friends,
and the story would grow with the telling. He must act
quickly and decisively to make sure there were no more drugs
in the school.

Mouth set firmly, Hugh Roystone returned to his study.
Frances Bell was putting fresh flowers on his desk. Before she
could speak he said, 'Too soon for any information yet, I
suppose?

'Not exactly, headmaster. Paula Darby came in.'

'Yes. I saw—You mean, about Avelon?'

'Indirectly.' Frances had an excellent memory, and she repeated Paula's story almost verbatim. 'Of course, there need be no connection,' she concluded.

Roystone swore. 'I bet there is. It wasn't possible to question young Avelon properly, but he seems to have told matron he found an envelope of those wretched cigarettes in his blazer pocket. At first she didn't believe him, but he stuck to his story. It's just the sort of tale he would tell if Pierson had given them to him. Poor little sod, he'd see himself as defending his hero.' Hugh Roystone shook his head sadly. 'One might have guessed that Anthony Pierson would be behind something like this—either Pierson or Grey, or both of them. Whenever there's trouble they're almost always involved. Why, if they hadn't deliberately missed that train and arrived back late at the beginning of term, Sylvia would never have had that accident.'

Frances Bell made no comment. She merely asked, 'Shall I send for them?'

'No—not immediately, I think.' For a moment Roystone stared unseeingly at the roses on his desk. He'd never been able to tell Frances that he didn't like having flowers there, that they got in his way. He said, 'Get me Steve Leyton first. I'd like to know what he's got to say about the affair. And then I want to see Mark Joyner.'

CHAPTER 9

'Your inexperience as a master is no excuse, Leyton. You showed a total lack of ordinary common sense.' Hugh Roystone was withering. 'Didn't you realize it was your duty to report Pierson and Grey? Good God, man, you didn't even come forward immediately after Assembly this morning!'

'I—I—' As Steve Leyton hesitated, Roystone leant forward across his desk and regarded him steadily. 'Think of the consequences of your behaviour. If you'd told me as soon as you found Pierson and Grey smoking pot I'd have made an example of them at once. Then no one, least of all an innocent like Ralph Avelon, would have been tempted to emulate them—or had any opportunity to do so. This whole wretched business would have been avoided.'

'I've said I'm sorry, sir.' Leyton shifted uncomfortably in his chair. 'I confiscated the joints Pierson and Grey were smoking, and they swore that was all the cannabis they had. At the time I believed them, and I judged it best to take the matter no further. Isn't it possible Avelon got his from another source?'

'Possible, I suppose, yes. Probable, no. Unless you assume like Mrs Avelon that drugs are freely available all over Coriston.'

Steve Leyton was silent. He was quite aware he'd been stupid, but he liked Pierson and Grey and he still found it hard to believe they had lied to him so blatantly. He listened stonily as Roystone continued to comment on the damage done to the reputation of the school.

When the interview was obviously at an end, Leyton got to his feet. He moved towards the door, and by the time he reached it the headmaster was already opening a couple of files that were lying on his desk. Leyton drew a deep breath and turned back. He said, 'Sir, am I to take it that you won't be recommending me for a permanent position at Coriston? In other words, I shan't be here next term?'

'Yes,' Roystone said without hesitation and without looking up from his papers. 'I'm sorry, but could you expect otherwise?'

Steve Leyton's smile was enigmatic. 'Thank you, headmaster.'

He passed through the outer office, nodding to Frances Bell at her typewriter, but not speaking to her. Neither did he speak to Mark Joyner who, back turned, was staring out of the window, awaiting his interview. Joyner was worried. Unusually, Frances had refused to give him a hint as to why he had been summoned, but the reason wasn't hard to guess.

'You can go in now,' Frances said quietly.

'Thanks.'

Unconsciously squaring his shoulders, Mark Joyner went into the study, and took the chair to which the headmaster gestured. He listened to what Roystone told him. But he was frowning as Roystone came to an end.

'I must admit I'm not surprised about Pierson and Grey,' he commented. 'They're always trouble, in a sense. But I still think it's odd they should have lied so directly to Leyton and denied any responsibility for Avelon's escapade. Whatever else they are, I've never known them to be vicious. In fact, I've always found them—well, trustworthy, when the chips were down. They wouldn't be prefects otherwise.'

'They've never been in quite so deep before. Smoking cannabis is illegal, after all.' Hugh Roystone shrugged. 'And to encourage a small boy to do the same thing is wicked, inexcusable.'

'Sir, we don't know for sure yet that—'

'No. I'm about to send for them. And while they're here, Mark, I want you to make a thorough search of their study, and take another master with you as a witness. If they've any sense they'll have got rid of any drugs they have left, but we must make sure.'

Joyner nodded. He didn't like the idea of searching the study of two of his prefects, but he clearly had no option. He said, 'Headmaster, may I ask? If they did give Avelon the stuff—and I agree it seems very possible—what action are you thinking of taking? They've A-levels in a few days, and they're both leaving at the end of term.'

'I know, I know. But I have to consider what's best for Coriston.' Roystone sighed. 'Anyway the first thing is to talk to them and see what they've got to say for themselves.'

★

As usual, Tony Pierson was the spokesman, but Peter Grey acquiesced in everything his friend said. Their story was unchanged. They categorically denied giving Avelon, or anyone else at Coriston, cannabis or any other drug.

'Did Avelon know you smoked pot?'

'You make it sound as if it were a habit, sir. It wasn't.'

'Answer my question, Pierson.'

'He caught us smoking once, yes, sir. But I'm not even sure he knew it was pot. It was the same day that Mr Leyton found us. Mr Leyton came along about half an hour later.'

Roystone looked up from his desk. 'You seem to have been pretty careless,' he said sarcastically.

'Ralph Avelon never said that either Peter or I gave him the stuff, did he, sir?'

It was worded as a question, but there was a confidence in Pierson's tone that turned it into a statement. Roystone eyed him for a moment, and Pierson returned his gaze. Even in the present circumstances Pierson exuded an irritating casual arrogance.

Roystone opened his mouth to speak, but the intercom on his desk buzzed. Frances Bell's voice came through. 'Please, could you come into my office for a moment, headmaster. It's important.'

'Coming,' Roystone said. As he crossed the room, he added. 'For your information, Avelon says he found an envelope of cigarettes in his blazer pocket. I find this somewhat difficult to believe. Perhaps he's trying to protect someone.'

If, by this last remark, Roystone intended to give the two boys food for thought, they had little time to digest it. The headmaster was back in his study almost immediately. He held in his hand a small cardboard box. Without speaking he emptied its contents on to his desk—half a dozen brown, irregularly-rolled cigarettes.

'You're a pair of liars,' he said abruptly. He was angry with himself as well as with them; he had so nearly believed them. 'You told Mr Leyton you had no more. You told me you had no more. What do you call these? They've just been found in your room, hidden at the back of a bookshelf. You didn't even bother to make a real effort to conceal them. You don't care a damn, do you? About Avelon or the reputation of the school or anything.' There was contempt in Hugh Roystone's voice. 'All you care about is enjoying yourselves.'

'That's not true, sir—what you just said.' Pierson had gone white, but he was not in the least intimidated by the headmaster's anger. 'Those smokes aren't ours.' He said it again. 'I repeat, those smokes are not ours. They can't be. Can they, Peter?'

Grey shook his head. He swallowed hard. He stared as if fascinated at the brown tubes on the desk.

'How do you suggest they got in your bookcase, then?'

'I've no idea, sir.'

'Someone put them there, I suppose?'

'I've no idea, sir. We've no idea.'

Hugh Roystone persisted, but made no headway. The two boys continued to deny everything except that they had, on a few occasions, smoked cannabis in private. But the circumstantial evidence was against them, quite apart from their reputations.

'I simply don't believe you,' Roystone said.

'That's your privilege, sir.'

'Don't be insolent, Pierson. It won't help you.'

'Sir, all we've done is smoke a few joints on school property. We—'

'*All* you've done? That alone is illegal. You think nothing of it?'

'I know, sir. But it's not exactly a major crime these days, is it? It's not like trading in heroin or robbing a bank or kidnapping someone or—'

They turned as there was a knock at the door leading to the Roystones' private apartment, and the headmaster's wife looked into the study. But Tony Pierson, carried along by the momentum of his words, and perhaps mentally cued by Sylvia's appearance, completed his sentence.

'—or having a little too much to drink and killing someone with a car.'

It wasn't till the words were spoken that Pierson was really aware of what he'd said. By then it was too late. There was an agonizing moment of silence.

Sylvia broke it. 'I'm sorry to interrupt,' she said, not looking at Pierson. 'I'm going into Oxford. There are some things I need and Helen's giving me a lift. We—we thought we'd have lunch there.' She smiled fleetingly.

'All right.'

Hugh Roystone heard the tension in his own voice, but he managed to return her smile. He put his hands below his desk. His fists were clenched, his knuckles white. He was thankful he was beyond reach of Pierson or he would have struck the boy. The door shut. Sylvia had left.

Pierson's superficial sophistication was unable to cope with the situation he had unwittingly created. He stood silent as Roystone said, 'I propose to expel both of you from Coriston forthwith. I shall telephone your father, Pierson, and inform him. As for you, Grey, since Brigadier Pierson is in charge of you while your parents are abroad, he will take responsibility for you too in this crisis, though I shall of course write to your parents at once. You will both remain in the infirmary until arrangements can be made for you to leave the school. Mr Joyner is waiting in the outer office, and he will take you to Mrs Cole now. He will also see to it that your belongings are packed.'

'But—but what about our A-levels, sir?' Grey blurted, after a glance at his silent, grim-faced friend. 'There won't be time to arrange to take them anywhere else. And I doubt if they'll have me at Oxford without them—not with an expulsion. I don't know about Tony. He's going to be a scholar, but—'

'I shall be writing to the Principal of the college you were both hoping to go up to,' Roystone said ambiguously. 'That is all.' He flicked the switch on his intercom. 'Ask Mr Joyner to come in, please, Miss Bell.'

Helen Quarry and Sylvia Roystone had a pleasant day in Oxford. They shopped and lunched and strolled through Christ Church meadows. Inevitably they discussed the disastrous result of little Avelon's experiment with cannabis, and the part apparently played in the affair by Pierson and Grey.

Helen was not sympathetic towards the older boys. 'It was wicked of them to give the stuff to Ralph,' she said. 'The child was really ill.' Suddenly she laughed. 'Poor Mark Joyner! As I told you, I met him going to tell Hugh he'd found more of the cigarettes in the study Pierson and Grey share. He was dreadfully upset. He feels responsible, and he is; all the boys involved are in his house.'

'What will happen to them? Pierson and Grey, I mean?' Sylvia asked as they walked down the broad tree-lined avenue towards the river.

'I don't know. It's all a bit difficult. They ought to be punished, but they're leaving Coriston in a few weeks, and next term they'll be up here, at Oxford, no longer schoolboys.'

'Hugh won't expel them?'

'Oh no,' Helen said with certainty. 'They have to take their A-levels next week.'

It was after six when the two women returned to Coriston, and Helen Quarry suggested a glass of sherry. Carrying a pile of parcels, Sylvia followed Helen along the corridor to the Quarrys' apartment. As Helen pushed open the baize door that led into the sitting-room they heard raised voices, and John Quarry said, 'It's no use, I tell you. The bloody man's made up his mind and he won't budge.'

There was a brief awkward silence. Then Helen said, over-brightly, 'What's happening? Have we interrupted a meeting?'

'More or less.' Quarry gave a wry grin. 'A sort of palace revolution. But one doomed to failure, alas.'

Helen laughed. 'What on earth are you talking about, John?' The three other men in the room, Mark Joyner, Simon Ford and Steve Leyton, had got to their feet. 'For heaven's sake, sit down, everyone.' She gestured to Sylvia to put down the packages she was holding.

'Perhaps I should go,' Sylvia said tentatively.

'No, you shouldn't. Come and sit down and let me get you a drink,' Quarry said. 'I've an idea. You might be able to help us, Sylvia. You see, your husband has decided to expel Pierson and Grey over this cannabis business, though it's not absolutely clear they've done anything except smoke a few joints themselves. Anyway, we've tried to persuade the head to change his mind, but he's adamant.'

'That's a polite way of putting it,' Simon Ford said roughly.

Helen frowned at Ford. 'Expel them? When? What about their exams?' She couldn't believe it.

'That's the point. They're to go tomorrow. No A-levels. At least, not here and now. And perhaps no university,' Joyner said miserably. 'And something to explain away for the rest of their lives. It really is too bad—especially without any real proof they gave joints to little Avelon or anyone else.'

'They've been a damned nuisance at Coriston in many ways, but we don't believe they deserve this.' Quarry gave Sylvia his most persuasive smile. 'The punishment should perhaps more nearly fit the crime, as they say. If you could help, my dear—perhaps use your influence with Hugh—'

CHAPTER 10

As the door of their apartment closed behind her husband, Sylvia Roystone sat up in bed. Her eyes were red from weeping, and her head ached. For much of the night she had stared into the dim light that filtered through the curtains and tried to smother her sobs, while Hugh, back turned, snored regularly.

It had been their first serious quarrel. The previous evening she had tried to follow John Quarry's suggestion and persuade Hugh to change his mind about the expulsion of Pierson and Grey. The headmaster had been furious, and had flatly refused. He had accused his wife of interfering in matters that were none of her concern. At Sylvia's unwise mention of Quarry's feelings he had at once accused her of ganging up on him with members of his staff.

'You've never taken much interest in the school till now,' he had said bitterly. 'Why pick on this issue—an issue you know nothing about?'

Sylvia had been stung into defending herself. 'At least I know why you're being so harsh with those boys. It was because of Pierson's remark about pot smoking being less serious than killing someone with a car. The trouble is he's right, of course.'

'That wasn't the point. He was suggesting you were drunk. Surely even you realized that.'

'Oh, Hugh! He was only repeating the old rumour. You can't punish him for that. It's not just. Everyone says how fair you've always been. They can't understand why you suddenly—'

'I suppose you gave them all a brilliant psychological explanation of my motives.'

'No, of course not. I—'

'Good! Because I don't need anyone to apologize for me, Sylvia—either to my staff or to the governors when they're here for Founder's Day. I'm quite capable of explaining my own decisions and the reasons for them.'

With that he had left the apartment, saying he was going out and might be late. She had heard him in the study telephoning, and wondered if he were making an appointment—a date—with someone, but pride had stopped her from trying to listen. When he returned, well after midnight, she had pretended to be asleep, just as she had done this morning.

It was all so stupid, Sylvia thought, as she got slowly out of bed and went to the window to draw the curtains. It was a grey day with a haze of summer rain, suiting her mood. She watched glumly as a group of girls, raincoats over their heads, ran laughing into College House, and she remembered the two boys in the infirmary; they would be as miserable as she was.

Turning away from the window, Sylvia saw the cup of tea on her bedside table, cold by now, a skim of milk on the surface, two biscuits in the saucer. She hadn't noticed it before, but now she was touched by the fact that Hugh had brought her early morning tea as usual, in spite of their quarrel. Tears filled her eyes and she hurried to dress, hoping to catch him after Assembly, before he became absorbed in school affairs.

But when she went through to the study she found only Frances Bell, arranging letters and papers on the headmaster's desk. The school secretary looked up questioningly. She noted Sylvia's reddened eyes, but made no comment. Nor did she feel much sympathy.

'I'm afraid Hugh's busy,' she said, anticipating Sylvia's inquiry. 'Brigadier Pierson's arrived already. He left London very early to come and collect the boys. He'd probably have been here last night if we'd been able to get hold of him or his wife.'

Sylvia noticed the plural pronoun, and wondered if Hugh had spent the evening with his secretary, but she merely said, 'Thanks, it wasn't important,' and began to close the door.

Frances called her back. 'I wanted to ask you about the governors' dinner party. Helen Quarry and I always arranged it in the past, but I assume you'll do it this year.'

'What governors' dinner party? I've never heard of it,' Sylvia said blankly.

Frances clicked her tongue in exasperation. 'The dinner party on the eve of Founder's Day, of course. Look, it's like this. The six governors always arrive after lunch the day before Founder's Day. They have their formal meeting at three o'clock in the afternoon. The chairman, Lord Penmereth, stays with the headmaster. The others are put up in the different houses. But they all dine with the head that evening. It's traditional.'

'Hugh's never mentioned it.'

'He's had a lot on his mind. And not as much support as he might have expected from some quarters, though I probably shouldn't say so.' Frances was tart, and there was no mistaking her meaning. 'The dining-room just about holds ten. The domestic—'

'Ten? What about wives? And one of the governors is a woman, isn't she? Has she a husband?'

'It's also traditional that the governors come to Founder's Day without their spouses. It was a little embarrassing some years ago when one of the wives had just died, and they decided that in future they'd be unaccompanied. The domestic arrangements—'

'Then how do you get to ten?' Sylvia interrupted.

'The Quarrys are always invited, and in the past I've acted as hostess, but obviously not this year.' Frances had arranged the letters and papers to her satisfaction and was about to leave. 'As I was saying, the domestic staff will cook and serve the dinner, but you'll need to arrange the menu well in advance. Some of the governors like their food—and their wines. And don't forget to order flowers and cigars. Hugh's a non-smoker and he always forgets the cigars.'

The telephone in the office rang, and Frances Bell hurried to answer it. Sylvia returned to her apartment. To her surprise she found that she was angry, her former unhappiness forgotten. She was angry at the way Frances Bell had spoken to her. She was angry with Hugh, who had put her in this impossible position by leaving it to his secretary to tell her about important events, and at the same time claiming she took no interest in the school. She was angry with herself for having so little idea of how to cope with an official dinner party. She had travelled a great deal with her aunt, stayed in first class hotels and eaten sumptuous meals, but at home they had lived very simply, and never entertained. Her anger gave way to bitterness. She was, she thought, a useless kind of wife.

Slipping on a light raincoat and tying a scarf over her head, Sylvia prepared to go for a walk. As she let herself out of College House, she was in time to see a Jaguar going down the drive. Brigadier Pierson was removing his son and Peter Grey from Coriston.

When the Brigadier had arrived, the headmaster was in the middle of taking Assembly, and John Quarry had been hastily despatched to meet him. Pierson was in his early sixties, a retired Guards' officer, tall and distinguished, now a director of several multinational companies. He was not a man to jump to conclusions. He listened to what Quarry had to say without comment, and then requested a private interview with his son and Peter Grey.

By the time the Brigadier had finished talking to the boys, Assembly was over, and Roystone was waiting. Pierson immediately asked to speak to Mark Joyner, and to see the place where the cannabis had been found. It was a demand rather than a request, and the headmaster felt obliged to cooperate, but when the Brigadier further asked to interview

Steve Leyton, Roystone refused to have him brought from the form room where he was invigilating an examination.

'All right. That's that, then,' Brigadier Pierson said decisively. He gave Roystone a speculative look. 'Headmaster, is there any chance I can persuade you to change your mind, and let Tony and Peter stay till the end of term, or at least until they've done their A-levels?'

All three of them—the Brigadier, the headmaster and an embarrassed Mark Joyner—were standing in the boys' study, where Pierson had inspected the bookshelves with some care. Roystone lifted his head, regretting that he was forced to look up to the straight-backed ex-soldier. 'None, Brigadier,' he said.

Brigadier Pierson's smile was bleak. 'In that case I'll wish you good day. I'm sure you must be busy, and Mr Joyner will help me collect the boys and their luggage.'

'Goodbye, Brigadier. I can only add that I regret this business as much as anyone, but my decision must stand.'

'And I can only add that I shall do my best to make sure you regret that decision, headmaster.'

With a nod, Brigadier Pierson turned his full attention to Mark Joyner. Roystone, somehow feeling himself dismissed, left the study with as much dignity as he could muster. He didn't altogether blame the Brigadier for his attitude—the man must be far more upset by the affair than he showed—and he discounted the threat implied by Pierson's parting words. It would merely be another complaint to the governors, but this time one that could in no way be justified.

Roystone had arrived at Joyner's house in Brigadier Pierson's car, so he was now forced to walk back to the main building. It was still drizzling, so he wrapped his gown around him, and borrowed an umbrella from a miscellaneous collection that stood in a large earthenware jar by Joyner's front door. His thoughts were now largely on Sylvia.

The rain, though slight, was sticky and persistent, and by

the time Roystone reached College House he was wetter than
he had expected. He left the umbrella in the front hall to be
returned at some future time, and was about to take off his
gown and shake the moisture from it when he saw, at the far
end of the main corridor, the figure of a girl leaning against
the wall.

Roystone wondered what on earth she was doing there at
this hour of the morning. Classes or examinations were in
progress throughout the school, or if she had a free period she
should have been somewhere studying or pretending to
study. Even an errand of some kind gave her no excuse for
propping up the wall. He shrugged out of his damp gown and
looked down the corridor again. The girl had gone.

Jane Hilman saw the headmaster mistily from her end of the
corridor. She had just come from the cloakroom. She had
been slowly and unsteadily making her way to sit her O-level
history exam when she had been overcome by nausea and
forced to run to the lavatory. She had tried to vomit, but
without success.

Sitting on the lavatory seat, eyes closed, feeling ghastly,
Jane had lost all sense of time. As the nausea slowly passed,
her head began to nod and for a minute or two she dozed.
Then, catching herself sliding to the floor, she had woken
with a start and realized dimly that she was late. She was
making slow progress towards the examination room when
she began to feel unwell again. Her knees almost buckled,
and she leant against the corridor wall, vaguely wondering
what to do. She saw the headmaster in the distance, and the
prospect that he might come and ask questions forced her to
pull herself together and stagger away.

As she came into the room heads were momentarily raised
and turned towards her. Steve Leyton, who was invigilating,
looked up from the book he was reading and said, 'Get on
with your work, everyone. You're wasting time.' He gestured
to Jane to go and sit at the one unoccupied desk by the

windows and, waving away her muttered excuses, added, 'Hurry up. You've already missed ten minutes.'

Jane Hilman walked uncertainly down an aisle between the desks. As she approached her seat she stumbled and knocked against Betty Farrow. For a moment Betty glared angrily, then her expression changed. She looked astounded. There were some nervous giggles and vague murmurs from the immediate area as Jane looked around and sat down heavily.

'Be quiet!' Leyton said. 'This is an examination. Get on with your paper.'

They obeyed. The exam was important to most of them. But the intense concentration which had pervaded the room before Jane's entry had gone. Those sitting near her seemed particularly disturbed. They fidgeted, coughed and cast surreptitious glances at her and at each other. Pretending to read, Leyton watched carefully.

Jane had turned over her examination paper, and was apparently studying the questions. She appeared to be behaving quite normally. But Steve was worried by the inexplicable undercurrent of unrest that he sensed in the room. Then he heard it—a sound, a sort of humming that turned into low, tuneless song. He could distinguish some of the words, and recognized the old nursery rhyme.

> 'Rock-a-bye baby on the tree top.
> When the wind blows the cradle will rock.
> When the bough breaks, the cradle will fall—
> Down will come baby, cradle, and all.'

There was no doubt about the source. Even the most dedicated scholars had stopped working. As one, they were staring at Jane Hilman, giggling, even whispering. 'Quiet everyone!' Leyton shouted, and the singing ceased. The silence was heavy.

Steve Leyton got to his feet and began to walk down the

rows of desks, looking over each shoulder. Everything was peaceful again, except that all eyes watched him as he came to the row beneath the windows where Jane Hilman sat. The unmistakable smell hit him before he reached her place.

Doubting his senses, he went to stand beside her, and leant over as if to read what she was writing. In fact, she had written very little. Her name straggled across the top of the page, and was followed by two or three meaningless phrases.

Jane turned her head, looked up blearily and burped gently in Steve Leyton's face. The smell of gin on her breath was revolting, and he had to stop himself from recoiling as she gave him a wide, unfocused smile. She was, he saw, quite drunk.

Leyton returned to his desk and sat, thinking. He couldn't send anyone out of the examination room to get help; it wouldn't be fair to the boy or girl he picked. And he couldn't go himself. This was a public examination and the invigilator couldn't leave the room. There was a bell for emergencies, but he was unwilling to push a panic button unless it were really necessary. He looked at his watch. Fortunately there were only ten minutes before the end of the school period. Then the corridors would be full of people, and he would catch someone at the door.

The ten minutes were long and slow for Steve Leyton, watching Jane Hilman anxiously. He need not have worried. Jane had abandoned any attempt to write, and had pillowed her head on her arms. Her fair hair hung down on either side of her head, covering her face, and her shoulders rose and fell rhythmically. She was fast asleep. Gradually she began to snore. It was a small, pathetic sound, and this time no one laughed.

CHAPTER 11

It was late that evening. In the Roystones' sitting-room, the headmaster was discussing Jane Hilman with John and Helen Quarry. Helen, who had been beside Jane's bed when she woke from her drunken sleep and had heard her sad story, was doing most of the talking.

'I feel so desperately sorry for the poor child. She's been worried to death the last few weeks and she's overwhelmed with guilt—she really is.'

'I wish I could feel as charitable as you,' Hugh Roystone said grimly. He rose mechanically to take the tray as the door opened and Sylvia brought in tea and biscuits; no one quite knew why, but they had all seemed to agree that tea was more appropriate for the occasion than alcohol. Hugh and Sylvia had had no opportunity to resolve their earlier quarrel, but they were both behaving as if it had never happened, though there was a certain coolness in their exchange of smiles. 'The girl allowed herself to get pregnant,' Roystone went on. 'Presumably she's never heard of the pill. But she doesn't go to her parents or a doctor or a clinic. She comes back to Coriston, takes boiling hot baths, steals gin, practically wrecks an important examination by getting blind drunk, and all because she wants to get rid of the brat.'

'Hugh, it's not unreasonable,' Helen protested, 'not given Jane's circumstances. They're all old-fashioned remedies, you know; old wives' tales, you might call them. I'm only thankful she didn't try a knitting needle or something.' Hugh Roystone looked up sharply as if he thought this remark was not in the best of taste. He was about to open his mouth but Helen persisted. 'Jane had no means of getting hold of the pill. You know the Hilmans live in the depths of the country, nowhere near any kind of clinic. And she didn't dare ask her

doctor for contraceptives or go to him afterwards. He'd have
told her parents at once, she says, and they'd have killed
her.'

'Metaphorically speaking, I hope,' Quarry said. 'Because
they're going to have to cope now.' He glanced at Helen.
'There's no doubt, I assume?'

'None at all. Dick Band's a good doctor and he was
positive. Either Jane has a proper abortion or she's going to
have a baby. Hot baths and gin won't help.'

'So,' said Quarry again, 'what *are* the parents going to
do?'

'That's easy. They'll come storming up here and blame
the school.' Roystone was bitter. 'First, Mrs Avelon. Then
Brigadier Pierson. Now, the Hilmans and they're likely to be
the worst. Why the hell did it have to happen to Jane
Hilman? Why not to some girl whose parents live in the real
world and aren't throw-backs to Victorian times? It could be
a disaster for Coriston, you must see that. The drug business
was bad enough, but Jane Hilman's only just sixteen. She
must have been under age when she started playing around.
And the Hilmans will hold the school responsible—and
rightly, too. We could get an enormous amount of adverse
publicity as a result.'

'For heaven's sake, Hugh, it happens from time to time in
all coeducational schools,' Helen said. 'And outside schools,
too. After all, we don't even know that one of the boys here is
responsible. As I told you, she absolutely refuses to say
anything about the father.'

'She must be made to.' Roystone was on his feet now, and
pacing up and down the carpet. 'If it's someone she met in
the holidays, then Coriston can't be blamed.' He paused. 'I
suppose that's improbable considering the way the Hilmans
live, but it's possible and for the good of the College we've got
to explore every avenue—'

There was a sharp click as Sylvia replaced her cup in its
saucer. She looked angrily at her husband, her colour high,

her eyes very bright. 'Damn Coriston!' she said. 'All you think of is Coriston College. What you ought to be thinking about is the girl and what's going to happen to her. And then there are those boys—Pierson and Grey. Have you done what's best for them? Even poor little Avelon— his mother's going to swamp him more than ever now. She'll never send him to boarding-school again, and a school away from her influence is just what he needs. You—you—'

Sylvia stopped, tears choking her voice. She was aware, of course, that her outburst was in a sense a continuation of her overnight quarrel with Hugh, though that didn't change her feelings. But she controlled herself, and said, 'I'm sorry. I know it's none of my business. Co—ris—ton, "Corston" as you call it, is your world; I'm not sure it's mine.'

The presence of the Quarrys was forgotten as Hugh replied heatedly and accusingly. 'You've never tried to make it yours—' he began.

'You've never given me much chance. It was only today I learnt that it's traditional for the headmaster to give a dinner for the governors on the eve of Founder's Day. And who had to tell me? Frances Bell—that's who.'

'The dinner—yes.' Roystone frowned. 'You're right there. I should have warned you myself. I'm sorry, Sylvia. I forgot. There've been so many things recently.'

'Anyway, the party's nothing to worry about,' Quarry said heartily. 'Just leave it in the capable hands of Helen and Frances. They'll produce a splendid banquet. They always do.'

Sylvia looked at him unsmilingly. She wasn't sure if he'd spoken unwittingly or with deliberate malice. 'That's precisely what I'm thinking of doing,' she said.

'We'll help, of course.' Helen was quick to try to cover her husband's apparent tactlessness. 'Just tell us when you want to have a natter, discuss the menu and all that. The whole thing was getting a bit stilted; I'm sure you'll have lots of new ideas.'

'Thank you.' Sylvia stood up without looking at either of
the Quarrys. 'If you'll excuse me, I'm going to bed. It's late
and I've a slight headache.'

There was a small flurry as she went, expressions of
concern, wishes for a good night. But, as she closed the door
behind her, she heard John Quarry say, 'I hope your Sylvia's
not going to suggest dancing girls at the dinner, Hugh, or
strip poker afterwards.' And she thought she heard her
husband laugh at the suggestion.

The Quarrys left soon afterwards, and Hugh Roystone went
into his study. He felt tired and depressed, but restless too.
He knew it would be useless to go to bed; he would never
sleep and Sylvia, he was sure, was in no mood to let him make
love to her. He decided to draft a letter to the Hilmans.

A letter was gentler than a phone call as a way of breaking
the bad news to them, and it would give the girl a little more
time to prepare herself to face them. In spite of Sylvia's
words, he did care about Jane. She was a clever girl, pretty,
attractive and in the past always helpful in the life of the
school. He hated to think what attitude her embittered
parents might take, how they might react.

It wasn't an easy letter to write. He couldn't be too blunt.
He had to approach the subject circumspectly, but if he
implied that Jane had been causing concern earlier in the
term the Hilmans would want to know why they had not
been informed before. He tore up his notes and started again.

He could forget about the hot bath incident, but he would
have to mention gin, not perhaps the bottle broken on the
stairs, but certainly the scene in the examination room. It
was the latter that had brought the whole mess out into the
open, and there was no way it could be avoided. In any case it
might be better to be frank with the Hilmans, who would
certainly want to know how their daughter had got hold of
the liquor. After some thought, Roystone wrote, 'Sent by her
English mistress, Miss Darby, to fetch a book from her room,

Jane saw a bottle of gin, and was tempted to take it, hoping that—'

Roystone stopped once again, sighed, crumpled the paper into a ball and threw it into the waste-paper basket. That wouldn't do either. It implied that Paula had been to blame for leaving bottles around, which was grossly unfair. Nearly all the staff kept liquor in their rooms, and with every right. There had never been any trouble before.

Then an idea occurred to him. If he could get hold of the cousin who had suggested that Jane should come to Coriston in the first place, and had herself inspected the school, she might be prepared to act as a kind of go-between. He remembered her as a pleasant, sensible woman who might also be able to help the girl, but he didn't remember her name. He was sure it wasn't Hilman.

Naturally there had been correspondence, and Roystone spent some time looking through the files in Frances Bell's office, but the system defeated him, and eventually he abandoned his search. Frances would find what he wanted in the morning, and he would contact the cousin. The cousin could be the solution to a lot of problems.

There still remained the question of the baby's father. Was he one of the boys at Coriston or, God forbid, even one of the masters? Jane would have to name him. And then what? Another expulsion? More irate parents? Roystone swore softly to himself. It was being a ghastly term. He couldn't remember any previous term in the course of his career that had been so beset by troubles. The high hopes with which it had started somehow made the present situation worse.

By now it was almost two o'clock in the morning. Yawning, Roystone returned to his apartment. Sylvia was asleep. She was breathing heavily and didn't stir when he put on the bedside lamp. He guessed that she had taken a sleeping pill. For a moment he stood looking down at her, thinking how much he loved her, blaming himself for his anger, resolving to be more considerate. Then, because she looked so tired and he didn't want to wake her when he got up in a few hours' time, he collected the alarm clock and his pyjamas, put out the light and went to sleep in the spare room.

Hugh Roystone's fingers grazed the tiled wall of the swimming pool. He turned and kicked and experienced a sense of exhilaration as his body surged through the water. He swam as fast as he could, urging himself to greater effort. This was the last length, and it was with a feeling of triumph that he reached his goal and clung to the edge of the pool. He was panting heavily, but he knew he had swum well this morning, in spite of his short night. It didn't matter in the least that there was no one to see, no one to admire; he was at one and the same time totally relaxed and totally invigorated. He pulled himself out of the water and ran for the showers.

Fifteen minutes later he was back in the kitchen of his apartment in College House, and the kettle had begun to sing. He made the tea, and poured Sylvia's at once, not strong, a little milk, no sugar. He added two biscuits to the saucer, Romary biscuits of which she was particularly fond.

In their bedroom the curtains were still drawn, but today the weather was good, the sun shining in a blue sky, and there was plenty of light in the room for Roystone to see at once that the bed was empty. The side on which he normally slept was neat and tidy, the other unmade, with covers thrown back.

Hugh Roystone put down the cup and saucer and went into the corridor. 'Sylvia! Where are you? In the bathroom? I've brought your tea.'

There was no answer. The bathroom door was wide open. The apartment was not large and it took no time for Roystone to assure himself that Sylvia wasn't in it. He went towards his study last, already convinced that Sylvia had chosen to go for one of her long, solitary walks.

He saw the envelope lying in the middle of his desk as soon as he opened the door. The letter inside was brief:

Dear Hugh,

I hope this won't be too much of a shock, but I'm
catching the early bus to Oxford, because I've decided to
leave Coriston—and you. I expect you can guess why,
though I'm not very sure myself. All I am sure of is that I
can't stand Coriston any more for the moment. It may not
be for good. I hope it won't. And I promise I'll be in touch,
so please, please don't try to find me. If anyone asks—one
of the governors on your Founder's Day, say—you can tell
them I've been called away to a sick friend.

All my love,
Sylvia.

CHAPTER 12

Hugh Roystone passed the next week or two in a kind of
personal haze. Bitterly hurt that Sylvia had left him, he
obeyed her request and made no effort to trace her. He made
excuses, lied and hid his unhappiness under an excess of
energy, determined that no one should know the truth. He
could imagine only too well the kind of comments that would
pass among the older boys and girls—and some members of
the staff—if it became known that their headmaster's young
wife had walked out on him.

Fortunately there was more than enough to keep him busy
at Coriston. Apart from the normal routine, the end of
Trinity Term, now fast approaching, always brought special
problems for the headmaster. There was his annual report
for the governors to be prepared; sporting events, at which
his attendance was desirable if not absolutely necessary,
seemed to come thick and fast; each pupil's end of year report
had to be examined and signed; all those who would not be
returning to Coriston in the autumn had to be seen person-

ally. Arrangements had to be made to interview candidates for the three staff vacancies, and the next term—months ahead though it was—had to be planned and discussed. All in all, Roystone was fully occupied. He worked late into the night, and tried not to brood over Sylvia.

The eve of Founder's Day came only too quickly, and with it the arrival of Coriston's governing body. The chairman was Lord Penmereth, a former Cabinet Minister. The longest-serving and most influential members were Sir Richard Stockwell, who was small and slight and looked a little like a jockey, but was in fact an astute businessman, the mandatory Church of England clergyman, the Reverend Horace Tanzel, and a Mrs Davina Carter-Black, whose late husband had been a major benefactor of the College. The two remaining members had been appointed more recently, and Roystone regarded them as nonentities, at least for the time being. It was the first four, he believed, that he needed to convince of Coriston's continuing well-being.

The governors met on time in the headmaster's study, as was their custom. Lord Penmereth took his place behind the headmaster's desk, while Roystone himself sat at the side of it. Comfortable chairs had been brought in and the remaining members were seated without formality. Unobtrusive at a small table in a corner, Frances Bell made notes for the record.

Lord Penmereth opened the proceedings by congratulating Roystone on his recent marriage, and expressing regret that they would not on this occasion have an opportunity to meet Mrs Roystone. Roystone replied briefly. The minutes of the last meeting were approved, together with a financial statement. Then Roystone rose to give his own report.

There was a short silence as he finished, and Lord Penmereth, in his rich, ministerial voice, said, 'Thank you very much, headmaster. Now, I wonder if you and Miss Bell would be kind enough to leave us for a short while so that we may discuss matters appertaining.'

'What on earth does he mean by "matters appertaining"?' Frances demanded as soon as she and Roystone had retired to the adjoining office.

'Complaints about the school being a hotbed of drug-taking and drug-peddling and sex and God knows what else, I suppose.' Roystone shrugged.

'Then why couldn't he say so?' Frances was indignant. 'Incidentally,' she added. 'I've not had a chance to tell you before, but the Master of your old college phoned this morning and said he hoped you—and Mrs Roystone—would stay with him while you're in Oxford for the Head-masters' Conference at the end of the month. I said I was sure you'd be delighted. I hope that's right.'

'Yes. That'll be fine.' Roystone gave a smile of genuine pleasure. Then his expression changed as he thought of the difficulty of explaining Sylvia's continuing absence, and of the meeting now taking place. 'That's if I'm still a head-master,' he said finally, 'and Penmereth isn't just about to ask for my resignation.'

'Hugh! You don't meant that? The governors couldn't—' Frances was aghast.

'They certainly could. But cheer up, Frances, I don't really think they will—unless there's some other catastrophe.'

'Heaven forbid! There've been too many already this term, ever since—'

Whatever Frances Bell was about to say was lost for all time, as one of the more recently-appointed governors appeared in the doorway and beckoned to them to return to the study. They filed back and resumed their seats.

Lord Penmereth cleared his throat, and peered at the school secretary. 'The gist of what we're about to discuss should be on the record, Miss Bell, but it must remain confidential, like all our deliberations. You understand?'

'Yes, sir. Of course,' said Frances.

The chairman turned to Roystone. 'Headmaster, we have been discussing the unfortunate incidents to which Coriston appears to have been prone this last term. As you probably know—or if not you can readily surmise—we've received a number of complaints from the parents of the children concerned, and from others who have become aware of these matters. We should now like to discuss them with you. We'll take them one at a time. First, the question of drug abuse.' Lord Penmereth looked around at his colleagues.

Sir Richard Stockwell began. 'Headmaster, what I'd like to know first is if you were aware, before the boy Avelon was taken ill, that you had a drug problem in the school?'

'I'm not aware of it now, Sir Richard.' Roystone was bland, if slightly equivocal. 'A single incident hardly constitutes a drug problem. But I assure you that until Ralph Avelon was found to have smoked cannabis and I learnt about Pierson and Grey from Mr Leyton, I had no idea that anyone in the school possessed drugs in any form—apart from those prescribed for medicinal use, of course.'

'Ah yes, poor Steve Leyton,' Sir Richard continued, smoothly changing the subject. 'I was hoping he would make a success of it here. His father's a good friend of mine, as you know. Don't you think you've been rather harsh with him? As I understand the issue, it was clearly a matter of judgement. You won't reconsider?'

'No, Sir Richard.'

'Very well. It's part of your contract that you should choose your own staff.' Sir Richard spoke without warmth. 'Miss Darby and Mr Ford are also to leave Coriston, I gather.'

'Both voluntarily, Sir Richard. Paula—Miss Darby— she's going to join relations in Australia, I believe. Mr Ford—'

'—hasn't been too happy here.' To Roystone's surprise, it was one of the newer governors—the nonentities—who intervened somewhat pompously. 'It's a pity, because I understood we were lucky to recruit him. He has high credentials, and I gather there are not many young men in the mathematics field who wish to teach. In fact, I've been glad to recommend him to another school of which I have the honour to sit on the governing body.'

'I hope he'll be happy there.' Hugh Roystone tried not to sound sarcastic. Ford was a brilliant scholar, he agreed, but he didn't fit at Coriston. His attitude to discipline sometimes left a lot to be desired, and he was inclined to become too friendly with his pupils. 'There is a kind of golden mean in these things, you know,' Roystone said. Then he added, 'I'm prepared to admit that my own relationship with Ford hasn't always been ideal. I think one must put it down to a clash of personalities. I wish him the best of luck in his new appointment.' The headmaster gave a slightly forced smile as he finished speaking.

'That's fair and reasonable. Such clashes can't be good for a school.' It was the Reverend Tanzel who intervened; he was a thin, seemingly acidulated man, but he spoke pleasantly. 'Now, Mr Roystone, I'd like to go back to something you said earlier. You mentioned one incident of drug abuse. Surely there were two: Avelon, and the boys who were expelled?'

'I consider them to be connected,' Roystone replied at once.

'Brigadier Pierson doesn't agree with you,' Lord Penmereth said. 'He swears neither his boy nor Grey would lie about such a serious matter.'

'There's no doubt they lied, sir. Their housemaster, Mr Joyner, found more cannabis concealed in their study.' Roystone hesitated. 'If it hadn't been for that discovery I might have given them the benefit of the doubt and accepted their word. They were about to sit their A-levels, as you're aware.'

'Think of the effect on their future.'

'Harsh, too harsh, headmaster, in the circumstances.'

'Especially as you had no positive proof they were Avelon's suppliers. Why, even if they did have some more of the stuff, the child could have found it for himself.'

'Coriston shouldn't acquire a reputation as a disciplinarian school.'

To this chorus of criticism, Roystone made no reply. Much of it he had already heard in similar terms from Sylvia, and its repetition had no effect on him. He waited, his face expressionless, making no attempt to defend his actions.

Then Lord Penmereth said, 'Fortunately, there's not too much damage done to Pierson and Grey. As you're aware, John Quarry was able to pull a few strings and arrange for them to sit their A-levels with the students of quite a famous London school.'

'What?' Roystone couldn't hide his astonishment. 'Quarry arranged that?'

'You didn't know?' Sir Richard Stockwell was amused.

'No,' said Roystone coldly. 'Mr Quarry hasn't seen fit to tell me.'

'How interesting.' This was almost the first comment that Mrs Carter-Black had contributed, though she had been following the discussion with bright-eyed sparrow-like attention. Unexpectedly she turned around in her chair and addressed Frances, 'Miss Bell, did you know by any chance that Mr Quarry had been instrumental in saving the day for these two boys?'

Frances Bell, taken aback by the sudden question, avoided meeting Roystone's eye. 'Why, yes, I did,' she admitted. 'Lyn Joyner, their housemaster's wife, told me in strict confidence.'

'It seems that a great deal goes on at Coriston of which you're unaware, headmaster,' Lord Penmereth said bluntly. 'And this leads us to the next subject—Jane Hilman. First, the girl has left the school and has gone to live with her mother's cousin, a Mrs Grantly, who happens to be a friend of Mrs Carter-Black here. We're assured she's in good hands. But she still refuses to name the father of her child, and before I left London this morning I received a letter from

Mr Hilman's solicitor threatening to sue the school on the grounds that the girl, while in the care of the school and below the age of consent, did become pregnant. I myself am by no means certain that such a case would stand up in court, but it could lead to a lot of scandalous publicity. I'll consult our own solicitors as soon as possible, of course—that is, if you all agree.'

There were nods of consent, and the discussion turned to the periphery of the Hilman case. Roystone was questioned about Betty Farrow's fall on the broken gin bottle, the occasion when Jane Hilman had fainted in her bath, the theft of gin from Paula Darby's room and the effect of Jane's drunkenness on the O-level candidates who had witnessed the scene. Whereas opinion had been almost unanimously against the headmaster on the expulsion of Pierson and Grey, he received no criticism on the subject of Jane Hilman. But the possibility of a lawsuit and scandal remained. And no one could doubt that the reputation of Coriston College— a reputation for which Hugh Roystone, as headmaster, was ultimately responsible—had been dealt a series of severe blows.

The dinner party for the governors that evening passed off more smoothly than might have been expected, though it scarcely began auspiciously. Frances Bell and the Quarrys had gathered in Roystone's apartment to await the arrival of the governors. Frances Bell continued to be full of apologies for having kept the headmaster in ignorance of John Quarry's arrangement for Pierson and Grey to sit their A-levels, but Quarry himself was the reverse of apologetic.

'Of course we didn't tell you,' he said bluntly to Roystone. 'We knew you'd never agree. But it had to be done. It would have been absurd for the boys to miss their exams.'

This potentially explosive little scene was interrupted by Lord Penmereth, shortly followed by the others. Drinks were served and they went in to dinner. The food was excellent, the wines well-chosen, and the chairman, now mellowed, proposed the customary toast to the school, congratulated Helen and Frances, and suggested a toast to them as a reward for their efforts. No mention was made of Sylvia, and it seemed to Hugh that everyone had completely forgotten her existence.

It was hardly to be expected that Roystone would enjoy the evening, though he made every effort to appear sociable and at ease. He was glad when his guests, apart from Lord Penmereth who was staying with him, had left. He offered the chairman a final nightcap, which Penmereth refused.

'There's one other matter I'd like to take up with you before I go off to bed and rid you of my presence,' Lord Penmereth said. He stood, legs spread, in front of the mantel, as if warming his bottom before a non-existent fire. His face was even redder than usual, though whether from wine or embarrassment it was hard to tell. He hesitated before speaking, and then said, with surprising gentleness, 'We gave you a bad time this afternoon, headmaster, but it could have been worse.'

Roystone looked up from his chair and shrugged. 'It's the governors' right to be critical,' he replied. 'And no one can deny it's not been the best of terms.'

Penmereth ignored the comment. 'Oh, there are always complaints. Funny, but people rarely write to say how pleased they are with the school—with anything, for that matter. But that's not the point. The thing is, I've had another letter—not a nice letter—which I think you should see.' He took a single sheet of paper from his wallet, unfolded it and held it out.

Roystone stood up to take it, and stared. His hand shook as he skimmed through the text:

the headmaster is a dirty old man—he pats us and presses against us—if he can get us alone he tries to touch us up—he pretends he is being like a father but it is horrible—no one likes it—it is worst for small fair pretty girls—please help us and stop it—having a wife has made him do it more—Coriston is becoming a dreadful school

The dashes between sentences had been added in ink, and most of the words had been carefully cut from newspapers or magazines. The name 'Coriston', Roystone saw, was from a piece of readily available school letterhead.

He recovered himself from his initial shock and thrust the paper back into Penmereth's hands. His voice was harsh. 'What do you expect me to say? It's filth! Utter filth! I'm damned if I'll bother to deny it.'

'I'm not asking you to.' Again, Penmereth spoke gently.

'And I'm damned if I'll deny the implication. Jane Hilman.'

Penmereth nodded. 'That's partly why I've not shown this to any of my fellow governors. People are apt to jump to conclusions. Add two and two and make five.'

'Then what are you going to do with it?'

'Do with it? Burn it, of course. Why not?' Penmereth took a lighter out of his pocket and held the sheet over an ashtray while he ignited one corner. When the paper was reduced to ashes he said, 'I could have done that when I first received it a couple of days ago, but I thought you should read it. In my experience it's best not to be ignorant of such attacks.'

'Yes, I suppose so. I've never—' Roystone sounded doubtful. 'I can't imagine who—'

'Someone did. The envelope was typed, by the way. It got destroyed by accident in my office, but my secretary noticed that it was postmarked "Colombury", so it probably originated here at Coriston. There are no restrictions on mail going out from the school, are there?'

'No.' Slowly Roystone shook his head. His first spurt of anger had subsided, leaving him drained of emotion. 'It certainly looks as if it came from here. It's revolting,' he added sadly.

'Anonymous letters often are. Don't worry about it too much. With luck this is the last you'll hear of it.' Lord Penmereth was suddenly brisk; he felt he'd carried out his somewhat unpleasant duty and he didn't want to discuss the matter further. 'Now I'm off to bed. Good night to you.'

'Good night. And thank you,' Roystone said. Thank God there isn't much longer, he thought. Tomorrow was Founder's Day, and Trinity Term was almost over.

Part Three

Termination

CHAPTER 13

'Attempted rape, that's all that's alleged! Not even an actual rape!' Detective-Superintendent George Thorne looked at his sergeant in disgust. 'Probably no more than a fumble in a car or a hand slipped down the front of a blouse. And for that the Thames Valley Police want to send you and me into the wilds of the Cotswolds. I thought we were meant to be part of the Serious Crimes Squad. The whole thing's absurd!'

Thorne pushed back his chair so that he could more easily lift his neat blue-trousered legs and put his gleaming black shoes on his desk. Speculatively he regarded the expanse of red sock now revealed. He was by no means sure that red socks were really suitable for working hours, but his wife, Miranda, had given them to him as a birthday present. Six pairs, too. They'd last him some time. He stroked his moustache as Sergeant Abbot coughed.

'I know, sir,' Abbot said, the soothing soft Oxfordshire burr clear in his voice. 'But there's a couple of points—you'll see them when you read the file. First, the chap that's accused is Hugh Roystone, and he's the headmaster of a coeducational school—quite a well-known school near Colombury—so a charge of this kind could do him a lot of harm. And then he seems to be a friend of the Chief Constable, sir.'

'I see.' Thorne ceased contemplating his socks, lowered his feet and reached for the slim folder on his desk. 'This school? What's it called? Coriston College?'

'"Corston"—it's pronounced "Corston", sir. Spelt Coriston and pronounced—'

'All right, all right. I'll believe you, Abbot. You should know. I was forgetting you're a native of those parts.'

Sergeant Abbot smiled politely. He assumed the Superintendent's comment was meant as a joke, but with Thorne it was difficult to tell. Bill Abbot didn't pretend to understand his Super. But it was hard to credit that Thorne didn't remember that his young sergeant came from Colombury, considering how recently they'd worked together on a case there.

'How far's this Coriston place from Colombury?' Thorne asked suddenly.

'Not too far. About twelve miles, say. On country lanes, though.'

'But I bet it's a long way from the sort of school you and I went to, Abbot. A posh place, isn't it? Not quite Eton or Harrow, perhaps. But your parents would need to be stinking rich to send you there.'

He's been putting me on, thought Sergeant Abbot. He's already read that damned file and put himself in the picture. Aloud he said, 'That's about it, sir.'

The Superintendent was frowning. 'But the little brats won't be in residence now, will they? It'll be their summer hols. They'll be off on Dad's yacht somewhere or gambling in Monte Carlo or driving up the Alaska Highway or peddling drugs in Katmandu, or whatever's fashionable nowadays.'

'Sir, when you—er—study the file, you'll see the incident happened after term and the girl—her name's Moira Gale—wasn't at Coriston.' Abbot tried to sound encouraging; he knew his Super's relationship with children wasn't always easy.

Thorne grunted and looked at the round face of the clock on the wall in front of his desk. 'Right. I'll have my elevenses early and get down to these papers. Then off to Colombury to see our old friend Sergeant Court, eh? Elevenses, please, Abbot.'

Wondering for the umpteenth time how his superior managed to keep his trim, military figure when he was so devoted to his food, Sergeant Abbot went in search of tea and sweet biscuits. Left to himself, Superintendent Thorne opened the file, glanced at the first sheet and shut it again. Sergeant Abbot had been quite right; he already knew the meagre details within it, and he wasn't pleased.

'Absurd,' he said aloud. 'Not my kind of job at all.'

He balanced his chair on its back legs and stared at the ceiling of his small office. The ceiling and the walls were all painted that shade of green beloved by public works departments throughout the United Kingdom. Thorne, on his arrival from London, had turned out the various kinds of non-flowering plants that had littered the room—its previous occupant had clearly been an indoor gardening maniac—covered the walls with maps and charts, and installed a square of dull red carpet around his desk. But the ceiling, and the memory of all that wretched greenery, continued to give him the impression that he was living in a jungle clearing, if not under water.

'Your tea, sir.' Sergeant Abbot returned with a small tray.

'Good.' Thorne looked more cheerful at once. 'Give me fifteen minutes, then we'll set off. Warn Colombury we're on our way, Abbot, in case the Sergeant's got a real job on hand. And the police surgeon, Dr Band. I'll have to have a few words with him. He examined the girl soon after this ridiculous attempted rape. And don't forget lunch, while you're on the phone. There's quite a good pub in Colombury, as I recall.'

'Yes, sir.' Abbot hesitated, debating whether to remind the Super that today was market day in Colombury. The town would be full and it might not be so easy to get a table for lunch at the Windrush Arms. He decided to leave it. Detective-Superintendent Thorne might be a difficult man to work with sometimes, but there was one thing in his favour: only in dire circumstances did he allow himself or his sergeant to miss a meal.

★

A warm, sunny day, market day, and Colombury had an air of bustle and excitement. The narrow streets, narrowed further by illegally parked vehicles, were chock-a-block. The pavements were equally crowded with women in bright summer clothes busy shopping, teenagers lounging in doorways, children, free from school, darting here and there, farmers seeking a quiet pint of beer before they returned to the cattle market. No one, except Superintendent Thorne, thought it in the least odd to see a man leading a young heifer on a rope through the main street.

There was, of course, nowhere to park, except directly in front of the police station, on a yellow line between two signs which read, 'Police. No Parking.' Thorne had hardly got out of the car before a young shirt-sleeved uniformed constable came hurrying from the building.

'Can't you read?' he demanded. 'It says no parking and it bloody well means no parking.'

Superintendent Thorne looked the constable up and down for a moment, grey eyes cold. Then, without a word, he walked straight past him into the station. Abbot was left to explain.

Once inside the building, Thorne's reception was distinctly less hostile. Sergeant Court welcomed him with the respect due to his rank, tinged with some apprehension. Court, though fully equal to his job, was a slow-moving, slow-thinking man. He had worked with Thorne once before, and secretly considered him brilliant, though he had had occasional reservations about some of the Superintendent's methods.

'I didn't expect you'd be coming down for this affair of poor little Moira, sir,' he said, after he'd seated Thorne and Abbot in the inner office.

'No more did we,' said Thorne, 'but it's a matter of who knows who. I'm told this man Roystone's an acquaintance of the Chief Constable. So you'd better watch out, eh?'

'Ah!' Court nodded as if he had fully understood Thorne's

comment. 'That's a pity, that is. Of course these cases are usually impossible to prove, but this time there were witnesses.'

'Reliable?'

'Oh yes, sir. Tom Ingle. He's the local butcher. And his wife and mother. All local people. They swear that if they'd not come along he'd have had her.'

'And the Gale girl. Poor little Moira, as you call her. Local too? Any relation to these Ingles?'

'No, sir. No relation. They'd never seen her before. The girl's not a local at all; she's never even been to Colombury. She was on her way to visit her aunt. It's the aunt—Edna Gale—who's local. She was born in Colombury, and came back here to live two or three years ago when she was widowed.'

'I see,' said Thorne. 'All nice and tidy.' He sighed. He could imagine the relationships, the local interest, the gossip. On the whole he felt quite sorry for Hugh Roystone. He let Sergeant Court ramble on while he considered his next move. Interview all these people, he supposed, but—

He interrupted Court. 'You say Moira was hitching a ride because she'd lost her purse in Oxford. Did she report this to anyone at the time?'

'Yes, the girl at the counter at Debenhams where she bought a scarf remembers the incident. I asked the Oxford police to check it out.' Sergeant Court sounded slightly indignant, as if he'd been found failing in his duty.

'So Moira set off for Colombury, hoping for a lift, and this Mr Roystone picked her up,' Thorne said.

'That's right, sir.'

'When was all this reported to you?'

'The same afternoon. The Ingles took Moira to her aunt and told her what had happened. The girl was very upset, of course, and she'd been knocked about a bit.'

'Had she? How do you know, Sergeant? Did you see her that day?'

'No, I didn't. But Dr Band did. Old Mrs Ingle insisted on calling a doctor at once. Dr Band treated the girl and thought she should stay quiet over night. But the Ingles came straight here and reported the matter.'

'Very public-spirited citizens, these Ingles,' Thorne said. 'Lucky for young Moira they were to hand.'

Sergeant Court nodded his agreement. 'I'm afraid it looks rather black for Mr Roystone, sir, if charges are pressed—by us or by the Gales. I might say little Moira's all against anything like that. She thinks the publicity would be horrible, and she's right. There'll always be people who'll say it was at least partly her fault. There's a deal of gossip already, as you can imagine.'

'You mean with every pound of sausages Ingle sells, there's a spice of scandal given away free?' Thorne smiled blandly.

Sergeant Court gave the Superintendent a dubious look. He was in Abbot's usual position; he wasn't sure whether Thorne was joking or not. As far as he was concerned, Mrs Ingle senior was a dreadful old harridan in some ways, but there was nothing wrong with the butcher or his wife, and they were all three of unimpeachable character. But Mr Roystone and that wife of his—Court remembered the fuss that Roystone had made over her accident. As if she hadn't been treated with every consideration—by the police, and at the inquest.

Court said stolidly, 'You can't blame the Ingles for the gossip, sir. There was plenty around before this, about the Roystones and about the school.'

'Was there now? There's nothing about any of this in the file. Tell all,'

'Well, Mrs Roystone—a nice young lady, much younger than he is—she was driving the school's minibus, and she killed little Billy Morton. There was no question it was a complete accident. The boy just ran under her wheels. But the Mortons were right upset, still are for that matter. I was talking to Frank Morton about it only yesterday.' Sergeant Court shook his head in sad remembrance.

When he didn't continue, Thorne prompted, 'You mentioned something about the school. Was that separate? Trouble at Coriston College too?'

Automatically Court corrected Thorne's pronunciation, and Abbot hid a smile. Court said, 'Nothing that's come to us officially, sir, though maybe it should have. I gather there've been problems connected with drugs and drink and under-age sex. Several boys have been expelled. But it's all been a bit hushed up, if you know what I mean. Dr Band could probably tell you more if you're interested. He's the school doctor as well as the police surgeon.'

'Is he indeed? That's a bit of luck,' Thorne said affably. 'A friend of Mr Roystone's then, I expect? Good. The head-master seems to need someone on his side—apart from our Chief Constable.'

Again Court looked at the Superintendent doubtfully. 'I'm not against Mr Roystone, sir,' he said. 'That wouldn't be right, not in my position, not at the moment anyway.'

'But you're sorry for poor little Moira?' Thorne didn't wait for an answer. 'Where is Band, anyway? You did tell him to expect us, Court?'

'Yes, sir. He said he'd be along as soon as his morning surgery was over. In fact, I can see him right now.' Sergeant Court was sitting beside the window overlooking Colombury's main street.

A couple of minutes later Dr Richard Band was shown into the room, a pleasant-faced man, beginning to go bald. However busy he was, he always managed to avoid the impression of haste or worry, both in his professional and his private life. He greeted Thorne and Abbot and sat down, leaning back in his chair and crossing one leg over the other as if time was of no importance to him.

'What can I do for you? Sergeant Abbot said it was about Moira Gale. You've read my report?'

Thorne nodded. 'Doctor, what's your opinion, off the record, about what happened between them—Roystone and the Gale girl?'

'I wouldn't dream of giving one, either on or off the record,' Band said instantly. 'I've known Hugh Roystone ever since he was appointed headmaster at Coriston. I don't pretend to be any kind of psychiatrist, but I'd judge him to be an intelligent, well-balanced man, quick-tempered some-times, but certainly not sexually deprived or perverted in any way. Actually, he's just got married to a rather shy but quite attractive young woman.'

'That's a pretty good character reference,' Thorne commented as the doctor paused.

'As for Moira Gale, I've seen her only twice. The first occasion was immediately—an hour or so—after the—the alleged incident. She had a black eye, which was swelling up, and several bruises and scratches, and she was slightly hysterical. There was absolutely no evidence of rape, and she didn't claim there was. I did the usual and gave her a mild sedative. By the next day she'd largely recovered, apart from the black eye, and she struck me as a sensible little girl. She's not unattractive, but she's got a child's body, small-breasted, not a bit sexy.' Dick Band grinned and sighed. 'Just anyone's young daughter. So you can take your choice, Superintendent. For once, I'm glad I'm a doctor and not a cop.'

CHAPTER 14

The Superintendent was in a good mood. When they left the police station he made unerringly for the Windrush Arms, even though Abbot had warned him that the restaurant upstairs was fully booked. 'We'll see about that,' Thorne had said, and of course he was lucky. He and Abbot had only just reached the top of the stairs, and Thorne had only just commenced somewhat acrimonious negotiations with the woman who seemed to be in charge when Dr Band appeared behind them. At once the atmosphere changed; it was simple to arrange for a couple of extra places at the doctor's regular corner table, and even simpler to order pints of mild and bitter.

The meal was excellent, if perhaps a little heavy for a summer's day and, having insisted that the ports with the coffee should be on him, George Thorne was feeling at peace with himself. He wished the doctor a very friendly goodbye, and agreed with Abbot that, as distances were so short, they should make their first calls of the afternoon on foot.

Abbot led the way along a short cut from Colombury's main street through to what had once been the village green, and then up a narrow lane to a row of ten cottages. Mrs Edna Gale lived in No. 3, which was indistinguishable from the other nine. Built before the days of plumbing and heating regulations, it was picturesque and inconvenient, and possibly not too sanitary. But it undoubtedly had charm, and Mrs Gale was overwhelmingly grateful that her late husband's insurance had enabled her to buy it.

Edna Gale opened the front door to the two police officers almost before they had a chance to knock. She had been in the front room and, peering through her lace curtains, had seen them coming up the path. She looked at them inquiringly, head on one side as if she were a little deaf and needed to listen hard. Thorne introduced himself and Abbot, and they showed their credentials.

'Police detectives?' Mrs Gale said, apparently in some awe. 'That's all right then. I was afraid you was more of those reporters wanting to question Moira. She won't talk to none of them.'

'But she won't mind talking to us, I'm sure, Mrs Gale,' Thorne said winningly.

'No, I don't suppose so.' Mrs Gale didn't sound as certain

as the Superintendent. 'She's in the garden at the back. She doesn't like to go out much, you know. She thinks people stare at her poor eye, even those who haven't heard how she was attacked. But it's a lot better now, and she ought to get out. I keep telling her. After all, this was meant to be her holiday.'

Mrs Gale led them along a narrow passage, through the kitchen and into the garden, which was bigger and more attractive than Sergeant Abbot had expected. Thorne, the Londoner, had had no expectations, and scarcely noticed the neatly mown grass, the bright border of flowers, the little vegetable patch and the hedge which gave the whole a semblance of privacy. Thorne's eyes were on the girl.

Moira Gale was sitting on a swing attached to the bough of an old apple tree, gently pushing herself backwards and forwards. When her aunt called she slid off the wooden seat, letting the tabby cat that had been curled up in her lap slip to the ground, and came to meet them. She was wearing a pink cotton blouse, the same pleated skirt she had worn when Hugh Roystone picked her up, white socks and sandals. Short—she was only an inch over five feet—small-boned and with a slight frame, she looked like a child to the two detectives; it was difficult to believe she was sixteen.

'Moira, this is Detective-Superintendent Thorne and that's Sergeant Abbot. They've come all the way from police headquarters in Kidlington to talk to you,' Mrs Gale explained.

For a moment Moira's brow puckered in a frown. Then, in turn, she politely took the hands the two men offered. Close up, the bruise around her eye showed a dirty brown-green colour, but she was quite composed. The description of her that Dr Band had given was, Thorne thought, very accurate. In spite of the two plaits which hung below either shoulder and her blue eyes, Moira Gale was no sex-pot, actual or potential. She was just a nice-looking little girl, anyone's daughter or young sister.

Mrs Gale installed them in canvas deckchairs on the lawn, and then surprised Thorne by leaving them, insisting that she had to visit a friend. The Superintendent turned to Moira, taking his time, not hurrying the girl. He asked about her home and her school and what she hoped to do when she left. She said she was an only child. Her Dad worked in a factory outside Reading. They'd be fine if he got overtime, but there wasn't much of that about. Her Mum, who wasn't strong, couldn't work and was just a housewife. Moira said she herself had got an odd job which helped a bit, and she hoped to stay on at school for another year or so and take some A-levels. Then, who knew? Perhaps she could become a secretary or something.

'What about getting married?' Thorne asked gently. 'A pretty girl like you must have lots of boyfriends.'

Moira agreed she would like to get married someday, but not until she was a lot older. At present, what with school and helping Mum and her job, she had no time for boyfriends.

Now Thorne changed the subject. 'Tell me just what happened between you and Mr Roystone,' he said abruptly.

Moira Gale drew a quick breath, and her fists clenched. 'I know what you mean,' she said. 'Nothing happened— nothing. He didn't have the chance. I struggled and the Ingles saw me and they stopped and he let me go. That was all there was to it.'

'But before that, when you first got in his car. Didn't he chat you up, try to touch you, anything like that?'

Moira shook her head. 'No,' she said shortly.

'Then why did you get out of the car?'

'He drew up and came round to my side. I didn't know why. I thought we might have had a puncture or something. Then he opened the door and said—I think it was, "Come along, there's a good girl," and put his hands under my shoulders and started dragging me out towards the bushes. I didn't even fight to start with, I was so surprised.'

'When did you start to struggle?'

'I'm not sure. Probably after he tore down the front of my blouse. It was then I realized—' She shuddered. 'It was all so quick and—and awful. I was kicking and biting and screaming. I—I'm stronger than I look and I was desperate. But none of it would have helped if those nice people hadn't stopped.'

Moira finished with a sort of sob and Thorne cast a quick, apprehensive glance at Abbot, who chose to ignore it. The Super had made her cry and the Super could cope. And Thorne's way of coping was to beat a hasty retreat.

'We must be off,' he said soothingly, rather as if he were speaking to a small baby. 'We're going to see those very same nice people, the Ingles, right now. Just to confirm your story. Not that it needs confirming,' he added hastily, 'but perhaps they'll remember some things you haven't.'

Moira nodded and swallowed hard. She had recovered herself quite quickly and managed to smile at Thorne. She told them she expected to stay with her aunt for a few more days, and showed them out.

'Whew!' Thorne said as they walked down the lane. 'I'd have brought a WPC if I'd known auntie was going to scarper like that.'

'It didn't matter, sir. The girl was fine.'

'Yes. She'd make a good witness.' Then Thorne surprised his Sergeant. 'Tell me honestly,' he said. 'Would you fancy her?'

'Me? Fancy her? Good God, no! I don't like wispy litle things.' Suddenly Abbot grinned. 'What about you, sir?'

Thorne paused, as if seriously considering the question. He said, 'I'm old enough to be her father.'

'So is Mr Roystone, sir. He's about your age.'

'That's just what I was thinking, Abbot. Odd, isn't it? And nasty.'

Abbot knew exactly where Ingle & Son, Butchers, worked and lived. 'I used to come here as a nipper with my mother,' he explained. 'Every Saturday, to buy the weekend joint. That was when old Jack Ingle was alive, of course. His missis—she was the old lady in the car—she runs the place now—and she runs her son and daughter-in-law, too. She'd run the whole blooming town if anyone'd let her. She's a fair tartar.'

The tartar, wearing her best summer dress, was waiting for them, sitting on a chair beside the cash desk in the shop. Rose was taking the money and, as Thorne and Abbot came in, Tom was obeying his mother's loudly expressed instructions and adding, a little reluctantly, 'A meaty bone for the dog' to an old age pensioner's stewing beef. There were four or five other people in the shop. Obviously, trade was brisk.

Mrs Ingle rose and greeted the two police officers by name, and there was a sudden hush among the waiting customers. 'Come upstairs, Superintendent,' she said, 'where we can talk in private.'

'Thank you,' Thorne said meekly.

Abbot avoided catching his superior's eye. Not sure if he was included in the invitation, he nevertheless followed Thorne through a beaded curtain, and up a flight of stairs into the Ingles' private accommodation. In the sitting-room Mrs Ingle gestured them towards an overstuffed sofa.

'I usually take tea about this time,' she said grandly. 'Would you like some?'

'I would love some tea,' Thorne said warmly, just preventing himself from adding, 'Ma'am.'

'Splendid. It's all ready except for boiling the water. If the Sergeant would help me with the tray—' Clearly enjoying the situation, she beamed at the two men.

'Of course, Mrs Ingle,' Abbot said dutifully.

With some difficulty he prised himself from the depths of the sofa and followed her into the kitchen, returning with a laden tray. Mrs Ingle waddled after him bearing a plate in each hand, one of buttered scones, the other of iced cakes. Thorne's eyes widened.

'This is a feast, Mrs Ingle,' he said. 'You must have been expecting us.'

Mrs Ingle almost simpered at the compliment. 'Mrs Gale—Moira's auntie—popped in to buy a couple of lamb chops for their supper, and I must admit she did mention you were talking to poor little Moira. I guessed you'd probably be along to see me.'

Thorne accepted a cup of tea and, pressed, took two scones. 'Why don't you just tell us what happened in your own words, Mrs Ingle,' he suggested. His mouth, he suspected, might be a little too full for a rapid exchange of questions.

Allowing the Superintendent to enjoy his tea in comfort—she had put the scones and cakes within easy reach—Mrs Ingle told her story. She liked to talk and it took some time, but in fact she was able to add little to what they had already read in her statement.

At last Thorne said, 'You say your daughter-in-law took the car's number. None of you recognized Mr Roystone?'

'No. We'd not seen him before, not to know.' She went on a little inconsequentially, sounding aggrieved, 'The school gets all its food from Oxford or London. They don't deal with us locals.' Then she said, 'But as it turned out we didn't need the car's number to identify him. He'd told Moira who he was.'

'When he did that he can't have intended to do her any harm.'

Mrs Ingle was shrewd. 'Well, maybe not,' she said, 'but think, he could have told her because he knew he was going to kill her after he'd raped her.'

Thorne acknowledged the sense of Mrs Ingle's reasoning. With some regret he refused a third cake. 'At the time, Mr Roystone denied there was any question of rape, didn't he?' he asked.

'Yes. "I didn't lay a finger on her." That's what he said. "Never intended her no harm." Those were his very words.'

Mrs Ingle gave a surprisingly crude laugh. 'And him with his trousers open and his shirt and his cock half hanging out!'

'You'd swear to that, Mrs Ingle? In court?' Thorne was suddenly very serious.

'I certainly would—will. So will Tom and Rose. There were three of us, remember, Superintendent, and we saw what we saw. It's only our duty to say so. Mr Roystone may be an important man, but it makes no difference. He should know better. And, as Tom says, if there's some kind of cover-up and he gets away with it, why shouldn't he try again? What'll we all feel when some other poor child round here's attacked and raped and murdered? And him being a headmaster—that makes it worse. What about all the kids he's in charge of—what chance'll they have if he tries anything at that school of his?'

It was a long speech and when she'd finished Mrs Ingle's ample bosom was rising and falling with indignation. Assuring her that the police were only concerned to establish the truth, and that there would be no question of what she called a cover-up, Thorne asked if he might speak to Tom and Rose. Mollified by his assurances, Mrs Ingle said she would go and send them up, but it would have to be one at a time, because of the demands of the shop. This arrangement naturally suited Thorne but, apart from a few unimportant details, their accounts of that afternoon's events tallied perfectly with each other's and with the old lady's. Thorne couldn't fault them on any material point.

As he repeated to Abbot on their way back to the police station to collect their car, the Ingles 'saw what they saw'. Hugh Roystone was going to have to face some awkward questions.

CHAPTER 15

Sergeant Abbot turned the car through the open gates of Coriston College, and guided it carefully up the long driveway. Thorne was slumped in the seat beside him. In spite of the excellent tea old Mrs Ingle had provided, the Superintendent seemed somewhat despondent, and had been silent for most of the journey from Colombury.

'I'm not looking forward to this interview, Abbot,' he said at length, 'not one little bit. I can see it's going to be very, very difficult.'

Abbot nodded his agreement. He couldn't think of a suitably tactful reply, but he knew full well that, whatever impression Thorne might choose to give, the Superintendent wouldn't be overawed by Coriston or its headmaster.

'At least there's someone to meet us.' Thorne sat up and smoothed his moustache as Abbot drew up in front of what was obviously the main building. 'That's a good start.'

Frances Bell came down the steps to greet them. Thorne had telephoned to request an interview, and Roystone had seen no reason to put off the evil. He stood up as Frances ushered them into his study, but remained behind his desk. It gave him an excuse not to offer his hand.

'You won't mind if my secretary stays while we talk, will you?' he asked as soon as they were all seated and Abbot had produced a notebook. 'I'd like a record for myself.'

Thorne was slightly surprised, but he got his own back. 'Not at all, sir,' he replied immediately. 'Of course, if you'd prefer, we'll go away and come back—tomorrow, say— when you've had time to arrange for a lawyer to be present too.'

Roystone smiled bleakly. He knew that his original request had sounded aggressive, and that the Superintendent had noted his attitude, but he didn't care. 'I don't think that will be necessary,' he said, and waited.

Thorne was now at his smoothest. He said, 'You know why we're here, sir. You've already talked to Sergeant Court. I wonder if you'd mind repeating what you said to him about the day you gave Moira Gale a lift. Then perhaps we might ask a few questions.'

'You'd like my version at first hand? All right.' Roystone drew a deep breath. 'I'd been attending a headmasters' conference in Oxford for a week, and I was driving back to Coriston—'

Apart from a less stilted choice of words, Roystone's tale was identical to the written statement already in the file, and up to a point it corresponded almost exactly with Moira's story. They even agreed on minor facts, such as that the girl had not run after Roystone's Mercedes when it stopped, but had waited for it to back up to her. Such facts, unimportant in themselves, all served to corroborate what the girl had said. It was when Roystone began to explain why he had parked the car and they had both got out that the two versions differed totally.

'She'd not spoken for a couple of minutes,' Roystone said. 'I was concentrating on the road—it was straight, but we were going through a wood and you know how distracting dappled shadows can be. I suddenly heard a noise like retching, like someone about to be sick. The girl had her head down and was fumbling for the window or the door, so naturally I did what anyone else would have done. I stopped the car at once—luckily there was a grass verge—got out, dashed round to her side, opened the door and tried to help her out.'

There was a long moment of silence. Hugh Roystone, his mouth set in a bitter line, seemed to be reliving the scene. Frances Bell, eyes downcast, was fidgeting with the papers on her lap. Superintendent Thorne coughed.

'The grass verge wasn't quite level; there was a slight drop away from the road towards the trees,' Roystone went on, 'and as she came out of the car she seemed to run down the slope. I went after her. I thought she was ill, of course. Sex, I assure you, was the last thing on my mind, and I was completely unprepared when she flung herself at me. I slipped and fell, and we both went down on the ground, struggling together. At first I got the impression she was trying to push me towards the trees.

'I know it sounds mad, me and that little bit of a girl.' He held up his hands, strong hands, with a few dark hairs on their backs. 'But she was stronger than you'd expect, and I suppose I was afraid of hurting her. It was a sort of contradiction. I was trying to hold her away from me, and she was clawing and biting. It wasn't until afterwards that I realized she'd got her hands in my trousers. I didn't even know that another car had drawn up till she leapt to her feet and ran screaming for help towards the people getting out of it.'

Roystone sighed. 'You've heard the rest. I now know the people in the other car were the Ingles, the butcher from Colombury and his family. Old Mrs Ingle promptly accused me of rape and murder and God knows what. They wouldn't listen to a word I said. I was so angry I just swore at them and drove off.'

'Straight back here, sir?' Thorne asked. 'You must have been very—upset.'

'That's the understatement of the year, Superintendent. I was angry and sick and—and dumbfounded—especially when I realized my flies were all undone. I could see what it looked like to the Ingles. But why, I kept on asking myself. Why? Why did she do it? Why me? John Quarry suggested it might have been because I was driving an expensive car, but—'

'Who's John Quarry?' Thorne interrupted.

'He's the deputy headmaster of Coriston. I met him and Helen, his wife, when I got back, and told them all about it.' Thorne looked up, apparently surprised, and Roystone said,

'Why not? They could see I was in a state, and they're good friends of mine.'

'It's not that,' said Thorne, 'but I don't quite understand. Term was over, but Mr and Mrs Quarry were still here. And Miss Bell, I take it? And your wife, of course—'

'No. Not Sylvia. My wife was—is—away. She's gone to look after a sick friend.' Roystone stared Thorne in the eye as if challenging him to question this last statement.

The Superintendent nodded, seemingly uninterested, wondering why Roystone had lied. Until that moment the headmaster had spoken frankly and freely—and convincingly. Now he was suddenly on the defensive.

Frances Bell said, 'If I might explain, Superintendent, the heads of the six houses, including Mr Quarry, live here all the year. Their school houses are their homes, as it were; they and their families all have private sets of rooms in them. Several of them were in residence at the time.'

The intervention had given Roystone a chance to regain any composure he had lost. He said, 'Would you like to speak to John Quarry, Superintendent?' and, when Thorne hesitated, 'Ask him and Helen to come over, Frances.'

It was not exactly how George Thorne would have wished to play the interviews, but he didn't object. When Frances Bell had gone into her office to telephone, he said, 'Once you'd got over the first shock, Mr Roystone, you must have reconsidered the whole affair. You said you discussed it with your friends. Did any of you reach any conclusions?'

'I've not discussed it much—just with the Quarrys and Miss Bell. It's not exactly the kind of thing one wants to make bright conversation about, is it? But I did write to Lord Penmereth, the chairman of Coriston's board of governors. I thought he should be informed of the situation. I've had no reply as yet. He may be abroad.' Roystone smiled fleetingly. 'But I've certainly given the matter considerable thought, Superintendent. Even if charges aren't pressed, the rumours alone could be enough to ruin someone in my position.'

'And your conclusions?' Thorne persisted, as Frances Bell returned to the study.

'None, really. As I see it, it must have been fortuitous. The girl couldn't have known I'd be on that road at that particular time.'

'Who could have?'

'Could have what? Known where I'd be?' Momentarily Roystone looked startled. 'No one could be sure. And the people who could make the best guess are from the school here. Everyone knew I was at the conference. There was no secret about the fact I was delivering a paper that morning, but had to leave immediately after the lunch to get back to Coriston to keep appointments to interview candidates for posts here. The staff would—or could—know about my movements, or any of the pupils if they cared to inquire, and perhaps some people at the conference. But surely not Moira Gale?'

'It would seem unlikely,' Thorne admitted. 'And what about the route you took?'

'It's the same story. It was well known I preferred the minor road, even though it might be a bit slower. We used to argue occasionally about which was the best way.'

'I see,' said Thorne thoughtfully.

'I did have one theory,' Roystone added after a pause. 'I'd told her who I was and I was driving a Mercedes. I wondered if perhaps she said to herself, "Here's a rich chap whose reputation's vital to him, so why not try a little blackmail?" But there's been no hint of blackmail—not the slightest. The girl's gained nothing from what she did—nothing whatever, as far as I can see, except some publicity, a lot of it probably unpleasant.'

There were sounds from the outer office, and Frances Bell got up to open the study door to John and Helen Quarry. Introductions were made, more chairs brought in.

John Quarry said, 'Superintendent, before you begin your inquisition I should tell you we're both utterly prejudiced.

We believe every word that Hugh, Mr Roystone, has said about this unfortunate business. Why that little Gale bitch should have told these appalling lies about him, we've no idea, but lies they certainly are.'

'Thank you,' Thorne said quietly. 'But what I really hoped you might help with was to join Mr Roystone in telling me about last term here. Rumours have reached the police of drug-pushing and—'

Roystone was suddenly angry. 'What the hell's last term got to do with it? We did have some problems, yes. It happens in any school. But the people concerned have all left now.'

'I'd like to hear about these—er—problems, sir.'

'Why? What possible connection can they have with the Moira Gale business?'

'I don't know, sir.' Thorne was conciliatory. 'Probably none. But it never does any harm to be fully in the picture.'

'Very well!' Roystone was still exasperated. 'There were really only two incidents, neither of them of any interest to you, but if you want to hear about them, okay. First, this so called drug-pushing. The Quarrys can stop me if they think I'm giving you an inaccurate account.'

Roystone explained briefly about Ralph Avelon. 'Pierson and Grey were both immediately expelled, Superintendent, though Mr Quarry, unknown to me, did arrange for them to take their A-levels elsewhere. And Mr Leyton will not be returning here.'

'You mentioned a second incident?'

'A girl became pregnant, I'm afraid. But I'll let Mrs Quarry tell you about her. She was in Quarry's house.'

Helen told them of Jane Hilman, with much sympathy. 'Poor child,' she concluded. 'Her parents are being dreadful, I understand—utterly unforgiving. I'm so thankful this cousin, Mrs Grantly, has taken the child to London and is going to look after her. By chance, I had a card from her—Jane, I mean—in this morning's post, and she sounded quite happy.'

'But she's never told anyone who the father is,' John Quarry said. 'At least as far as we know.'

It was perhaps a gratuitous remark, and Roystone responded immediately. 'I'll have to hope the baby will be blue-eyed and fair-haired like its mother, won't I? Then there'll be less incentive for anyone to suspect it's mine.'

'Hugh, no one's ever suggested that!' Helen Quarry protested.

'Haven't they?' Roystone turned to Thorne. 'As you're so interested in Coriston, Superintendent, perhaps you should know that the Hilmans are probably going to sue the school for not looking after their daughter adequately. The chairman, Lord Penmereth, will give you the details, I'm sure.'

'Thank you, gentlemen—and ladies.' Thorne said suddenly. He stood up. 'You've all been very helpful. I'm sorry to have taken up so much of your time.'

Hurriedly Sergeant Abbot put away his pad and pen and got to his feet. Once again he'd been taken unawares. To his mind, the Super had a habit of abandoning interviews just at the point when they were beginning to get interesting, and with some vital questions unasked. Thorne said he liked people to stew and, Abbot had to admit, the method paid dividends more often than not.

They said their goodbyes and Frances Bell took the two police officers down to the front door. 'Most unfortunate, this business, Miss Bell, isn't it?' Thorne said chattily. 'For everyone concerned. Worst for the headmaster, of course, but it can't be too pleasant for you or his other friends—or his poor wife. Where is Mrs Roystone at present?'

'Where—' For once in her life Frances Bell was completely at a loss. 'Where is she? But Mr Roystone told you. She's looking after a sick friend.'

'Very kind of her, especially when there's all this trouble at home.' Thorne smiled. 'I wonder—I should have asked before—do you have her address?'

'Her address?' Two ugly spots of colour had appeared on Frances Bell's cheekbones. 'You want Mrs Roystone's address?'

'It doesn't matter. It was just a thought.' Thorne brushed the question aside hastily. 'Goodbye, Miss Bell.'

Sergeant Abbot knew better than to interrupt his Super when Thorne was lost in thought, and they were three-quarters of the way to Kidlington before Thorne roused himself. He was looking pleased.

'We've got a hard day's work ahead of us tomorrow, Abbot,' he said. 'I hope you wrote all those names down carefully.'

'Names, sir?'

'Yes—Hilman and Pierson and so on. All the people who could bear Roystone a grudge for sacking them or expelling their sons or letting their daughters get pregnant or God knows what else. You might add John Quarry to the list. There's some sort of aggro between him and Roystone, whatever kind of face they put on it.'

'I've got all the names that were mentioned, yes, sir. But—do we really need them?' Abbot was puzzled.

'We might. Keep that list, Abbot, and if any others turn up, we'll add them. Because, as I see it, there are only three possible explanations for this affair.'

'Yes, sir,' Abbot said. Now, he knew, would come the exposition.

'Roystone could be lying. Perhaps he did try to make the girl. That's number one,' Thorne said. 'It's clear he's been under a strain. What with his wife's accident and the troubles at the school he's had a bad term. And now his wife seems to have departed. I'm not sure I believe in this sick friend. It's conceivable Roystone had a moment of aberration when he had the Gale girl in his car.'

'Alternatively, Roystone's in the clear and Moira Gale's

lying,' Abbot said, anxious to make a contribution.

'Yes. It could have been our Moira who acted on impulse,' Thorne agreed. 'A little blackmail in prospect, as Roystone suggested. Then maybe the Ingles made more fuss than she expected, insisting on going to the police and all that, and she decided it was wiser not to follow it up. Let sleeping head-masters lie, as it were.'

'But she'd have been taking an awful risk, sir,' said Abbot doubtfully. 'The chance she'd get anything from it would have been very slight.'

'Unless she was sure of a reward in advance, yes.'

'What do you mean by that, sir?'

'The third possibility, Abbot. Someone hating Roystone's guts. Someone who gives little Moira a hefty bribe to put on an act. We can't forget that. Which brings me right back to what I said. We've got a lot of work ahead of us. We need to know a great deal more about that girl, and about Roystone's friends and enemies. Still, tomorrow's another day.'

Thorne leant back and closed his eyes as they started to run into traffic near Oxford. A quiet evening with Miranda and the television was just what he needed, he thought.

CHAPTER 16

'Plans have changed, Abbot,' Thorne announced. 'This morning, instead of us dashing round the countryside look-ing for people, they're coming to us, or rather one is—but an important one. Lord Penmereth, remember—chairman of the Coriston governing board—he's calling in here on his way to see Roystone. He can tell us a lot about the school and the people. All arranged by our own Chief Constable, just for our convenience, of course.'

'That's great, sir.' As was so often the case Abbot looked at the Superintendent doubtfully, unsure whether his words

had a hidden meaning. What was more, Abbot was suffering
from the effects of a late night out with the boys, and thought
a morning spent driving through the countryside might be
preferable to one cooped up in an office. But he was thankful
that Thorne was in a good temper. 'When's his lordship
coming, sir?' he asked.

'Between ten and eleven. Meanwhile, I've got plenty of
paper work to occupy me and I'm sure you can employ
yourself.'

Dismissed, Abbot retreated to the staff canteen and drank
several cups of black coffee. But quite soon he was located by
a uniformed constable who said he was wanted on the phone.
The call was from Oxford. Moira Gale's purse had been
discovered by a cleaning woman stuffed behind a radiator in
a ladies' cloakroom in Debenhams. Needless to say, it was
empty except for a handkerchief, but the fact that it had been
found in that particular store was another point in the girl's
favour. Going in to Thorne's office to report this, Abbot
found that Lord Penmereth had arrived.

Thorne was at his most expansive. 'Ah, Abbot,' he said, 'I
was just about to send for you.' Then to Penmereth, 'You
won't object if my sergeant sits in on our talk, will you, my
lord? It will save me repeating whatever you have to tell us,
and he can take notes, if necessary.'

Penmereth nodded his agreement. His heavy jowls were
set in grim lines. 'This is a most distasteful affair, Superintendent, most distasteful. The sooner it's cleared up, and Mr
Roystone exonerated, the better. It's bad for everyone concerned, of course, but I'm mainly interested in the good
name of the school. We can't stand much more bad publicity.
I've been away—in the States on business—or I'd have been
agitating long before this.'

'It's not only a distasteful affair,' said Thorne. 'It seems to
me possible it may be rather a delicate one.' He looked up at
Penmereth. 'But I assure you we've wasted no time, sir. The
fact that your Mr Roystone was acquainted with our Chief

Constable helped, of course, but in any case—' He stopped
as Penmereth raised his hand as if to wave away any attempt
at apology, then continued. 'Now, my lord, there are questions I'd like to ask you which may seem irrelevant, and I
wouldn't wish to appear presumptuous—'

'Ask me any damn thing you like,' Penmereth interrupted.
'Let's just get on with it.' He reached into his pocket. 'Mind if
I smoke?'

'Not at all, sir,' George Thorne lied at once. 'Abbot, fetch
an ashtray for Lord Penmereth.'

'Yes, sir.'

Abbot, hiding his amusement, hurried from the room. The
Super, he thought, was going all out to soft soap his lordship.
Thorne was a dedicated non-smoker, and he hated others
smoking near him. As for not wishing to seem presumptuous,
that was a laugh. If the Super had questions to ask, he'd ask
them, presumptuous or not.

When Abbot returned with the ashtray a few minutes later
Penmereth was puffing at a large cigar, and Thorne had
opened a window. The conversation had clearly been in
progress ever since Abbot left, though the Sergeant found it
hard to imagine how it had reached its present topic so
rapidly.

'It's no secret,' Penmereth was saying. 'I'd have preferred
John Quarry as head, but the governors voted for Roystone,
and Roystone's done a very good job. Until this last term
Coriston's flourished under him.'

'This may seem an unnecessary question, sir, but you've
never had any reason to doubt his personal integrity?'

'Good God, no!' Penmereth paused. 'But if you ask me if
I'd swear to it, I'm not sure. Now, don't get me wrong. For
that matter, I'm not sure I'd swear to my own.' Penmereth
gave a barking laugh that held no humour. 'Let me just say,
from my own knowledge and judgement of the man, that I'd
be enormously surprised and shocked if he did in fact assault
this girl. And I've some experience of judging character.'

'That's good enough for me, sir,' Thorne said a little enigmatically, glancing unnecessarily at the papers in front of him. 'I see that Mr Roystone has been at the school for six years, Mr Quarry for two.'

'Yes. Roystone was keen to have him as deputy. Apart from anything else, they're old friends. Quarry had applied for another headship and been turned down. He's an academic and a good teacher, but possibly not such a good manager.' His lordship shrugged.

'Anyway Coriston—' Thorne had now accepted the general pronunciation of the name—'Coriston's done well, till last term. It's conceivable that the key to the case lies in the term as a whole, if you follow me. Did you agree with the way Mr Roystone handled the cannabis problem, Lord Penmereth?'

Penmereth answered without hesitation. 'No, I didn't. Fortunately, thanks to John Quarry, Pierson and Grey have sat their examinations, and the Oxford college they're going to isn't taking a serious view of the matter. But I think Roystone made a mistake, a bad mistake.'

'Would you care to elaborate on that, sir?'

Penmereth regarded the tip of his cigar for a moment, then said, 'All right. I've probably been exceeding my authority, but I've made some inquiries of my own, and I'm convinced Roystone didn't make enough effort to get at the truth. I paid a tactful call on Mrs Avelon, and I saw young Ralph. He swears he found the cigarettes in his pocket. I also talked to Tony and Peter—I know Brigadier Pierson, Tony's father, quite well—and they both swear they had no cannabis left after the episode with Leyton, and they certainly didn't put anything in Avelon's pocket. Personally, I believe them. So, you may be interested to hear, does their housemaster, Mark Joyner, though they were far from being model pupils, and it was he—Joyner—who actually searched their study and found the cigarettes.'

'But Mr Roystone didn't?'

'Believe them? No. Tony Pierson has a theory about that. He says that when Roystone was questioning them, he foolishly remarked that smoking pot wasn't as bad as killing someone by drunk driving. Roystone immediately took it as a reference to his wife and her accident at the beginning of the term.'

'But—' Thorne raised his eyebrows—'I understand she was completely exonerated. There was no question of careless driving, let alone drink.'

'None, but there had been a rumour going round the school, and Roystone may—must—have heard it.' Penmereth drew on his cigar and exhaled the smoke in Thorne's direction. 'Poor chap. No wonder if his judgement was a bit clouded. He's had a bad time.'

Thorne was about to agree, but the cigar smoke was in his nose. His eyes were stinging. He could feel a tickle at the back of his throat and feared he was about to have a coughing fit. Hurriedly he swallowed hard.

'Damnable things, rumours,' Lord Penmereth continued, oblivious of Thorne's plight. 'They can do untold harm to people—or to institutions like schools. This business of Jane Hilman's baby, for instance. You know about that, I suppose?' Thorne nodded. 'There was a story going round she was so desperate she tried to do away with herself. Quite untrue, Mrs Quarry assured me, but impossible to quash.'

For a few minutes they discussed Jane Hilman and her parents. Thorne had temporarily recovered from the effects of the cigar smoke and offered Lord Penmereth some coffee. Penmereth refused.

'No, thanks. I must be off soon, unless you've got any more questions. Incidentally, if you want to know anything else about the Hilman girl, Superintendent, you couldn't do better than have a word with Mrs Farrow. She's a gossipy woman, but it was her Betty who shared a study with Jane. The Farrows live at Blewbury, between here and Reading.

You can find them in the phone book, or get their address from Roystone's secretary.'

'Thank you, my lord, we might do that.'

'Though I can't imagine what any of this might prove, except to show that Roystone's been under a considerable strain recently.'

'Probably nothing, but you never know.' Thorne paused as if to change the subject. 'There are a couple more questions I have to ask, my lord. Do you know of anyone who might have a grudge against Mr Roystone or against Coriston itself?'

'Well, to start with, the Hilmans think they have, don't they? They're threatening to sue, as I said. Possibly the Piersons, too, though I'd find it hard to believe that Brigadier Pierson would—' Lord Penmereth had been quick to follow Thorne's train of thought. 'There's Steve Leyton, too. He lost his job at Coriston for not reporting the pot smokers. Simon Ford's leaving voluntarily at the end of term, but he didn't get on with Roystone any too well. My dear Superintendent, there could be dozens of potential enemies. Aren't you clutching at straws?'

'Possibly, sir.'

'Then what about the Mortons, the Colombury couple whose son was killed? They could conceivably have some connection with Moira Gale, and they could imagine they've got a reason for hating the Roystones—even the school.'

'I've not forgotten them, Lord Penmereth, but we've not had an opportunity to speak to everyone as yet.' Thorne flicked through the papers on his desk again. 'Just one more thing. To your knowledge, has anyone suggested that Mr Roystone could be the father of Jane Hilman's child?'

Surprisingly, Lord Penmereth took his time before answering. Slowly and carefully he stubbed out his cigar. Concentrated on what he was doing, he missed Thorne's disapproving sniff. At last he said, 'Perhaps you should

know, Superintendent. Some time ago I received an anonymous letter, posted in Colombury. I showed it to Roystone.
It accused him of—of touching up his pupils, as they say,
especially if they were fair and pretty. The description
would, I gather, fit Jane Hilman.'

'Where's the letter now, sir?' asked Thorne. 'Can we see
it?'

'No. I burnt it in front of Roystone. He was revolted, and it
seemed the fair thing to do.'

'Can you describe it, my lord?'

'It was the usual sort of thing. Words cut out of newspapers and pasted on a bit of paper. My secretary noticed the
envelope was postmarked Colombury. Oh, and one word—
Coriston—had been cut from the school's letterhead, so it
certainly looked as if it came from here.'

'I see, sir,' murmured Thorne thoughtfully. 'Fair and
pretty, you said, my lord? That description could fit Moira
Gale too.'

'Could it now?' Lord Penmereth said. 'I didn't know that.'
He swore softly.

Ten minutes later Lord Penmereth had been shown out of
the Kidlington police headquarters by Superintendent
Thorne, and Abbot, having removed the offending ashtray,
was flapping a newspaper in an effort to clear the
atmosphere.

'Elevenses, sir?' he asked as Thorne returned.

'No,' Thorne grunted. 'It's too late, and this room isn't
habitable. Get me Mrs Farrow's address and phone number.
I'll call her and if she'll see us we'll get along to Blewbury,
stopping for a pint en route.'

Bill Abbot grinned. The Super might have some odd little
ways, but there was a lot to be said for him. It was a warm,
sunny day, and a drive and a pint would be just the thing. His
headache had gone, and he was feeling in reasonable form
again.

'Yes, sir,' he said. 'I know a splendid pub—'

'You always do,' Thorne said absently. His mind was on the case. It was true enough, he thought. Someone might have put those joints in the Avelon kid's pocket. Someone other than the two boys might have hidden the joints in their study. Those rumours might not have started spontaneously. Certainly someone must have sent Penmereth that letter. It didn't have to be the same someone in each case, but . . . He had the beginnings of a theory, all right, but it wouldn't be easy to prove. He sighed, knowing only too well the danger of trying to make facts fit a preconceived idea.

As Lord Penmereth had said, Mrs Farrow talked too much, but that suited Thorne. Experience had taught him that the most seemingly irrelevant remarks were often of value. And Mrs Farrow was shrewd after her fashion, and nobody's fool. She'd apparently been delighted to accept without question their explanation that they were making inquiries relating to the illegal use of cannabis at Coriston but the gossip ranged widely. The only trouble was that Mrs Farrow monopolized the conversation. Betty Farrow, whose impressions and opinions Thorne was really seeking, had remained in what was probably, in the presence of her mother, an accustomed near-silence, kicking her heels against the base of a garden urn.

'. . . not really suitable for a headmaster's wife,' Mrs Farrow was saying. 'Not kind and motherly, like Mrs Quarry.' She was talking about her meeting with Sylvia Roystone at the Randolph in Oxford. 'You'd have expected her to know about Betty's ankle. One hopes it isn't every day at Coriston that a pupil falls over a broken bottle of gin on the stairs. But of course she's very young. I can't think why men who marry in middle age always pick on young girls. It makes one wonder what they did before—' She broke off, her comment unfinished, as Betty Farrow muttered something.

The four of them, the two detectives, Mrs Farrow and her daughter, were sitting on the Farrows' patio. The sun was warm, the sound of the gardener's lawn-mower soporific and, after a short night, no breakfast and a pint of mild and bitter, Sergeant Abbot was half asleep. But George Thorne wasn't. His sharp ears had caught the gist of Betty's murmur.

'You don't like Coriston much, Miss Farrow?'

Betty looked up in surprise. She hadn't expected anyone to hear what she'd said and she wasn't used to being called 'Miss Farrow'. Usually, no one paid her any attention, especially when her mother was talking.

'Not much,' she agreed. 'Last term was dreadful. I'd like to leave, but Daddy won't let me.'

'Certainly not,' Mrs Farrow said. 'You're only sixteen. You're much too young. Besides you only want to leave because Miss Darby's going.'

'Jane's left.'

'Do be sensible, Betty. Jane had to go. You wouldn't want to leave for the same reason, I hope.' Mrs Farrow turned back to Thorne. 'You know about Jane Hilman, Superintendent?'

'Yes, Mrs Farrow. I was wondering if your daughter could tell me anything about her. I know about Miss Hilman's pregnancy and her parents' reaction, but I thought that, as the two girls shared a room, perhaps—'

'I doubt if Betty can help you much, Superintendent. They may have shared a room, but they weren't such good friends, were you, Betty?'

'I suppose not,' said Betty, as if considering the matter seriously for the first time. 'She wasn't the sort of girl to make real friends with—not the sort of girl who'd tell you everything. But—'

'But what?' said Thorne immediately. 'You've no idea at all who the father might be, have you, Miss Farrow?

'N-no—' Betty paused, looking at Thorne, glad to be the

centre of attraction. 'But actually I don't believe it was anyone at Coriston at all.'

'Betty! You've never said that before.' This from her mother.

'No one's ever asked me. And besides it's different when it's the police. Anyway, I don't know for sure. What I do know is that Jane was sort of odd when she came back after the Easter holiday.' Betty glanced at her mother and the two men in slight embarrassment. 'She was worried when she missed her—her period the first week of term. Later she said it was all right, but that must have been a fib.'

'This is important, you know, Miss Farrow,' said Thorne. 'That information could clear the school of any responsibility. Lord Penmereth would be pleased. And it could help to persuade Jane Hilman to name the man.' He gave Betty his most pleasant smile. 'It could also stop a lot of gossiping and guessing about—'

'—about Mr Roystone,' Betty interrupted.

'Betty!' This time Mrs Farrow was genuinely shocked.

'Why not? He—he touched me up once in the swimming pool. He was pretending to help me do a duck dive and he put his hand up between my legs. It was horrid.'

'But—' For once, Mrs Farrow was at a loss for words. 'Betty, are you sure you didn't imagine it?'

'I knew you'd say that,' her daughter said triumphantly. 'That's why I didn't tell you. Actually, it's what Miss Darby said too—that I must have imagined it. As for Jane, all she said was that if Mr Roystone wanted to touch anyone up he'd choose someone more attractive than me.'

'And you didn't mention this—er—incident to anyone else?' Thorne said. 'Your housemistress, say?'

'Mrs Quarry, you mean. She's not my housemistress. She's my housemaster's wife. No.' Betty Farrow shook her head. 'If I couldn't convince Miss Darby, I didn't think I'd convince anyone.'

'Betty thinks the world of Miss Darby,' Mrs Farrow said

quickly, glad of an opportunity to change the subject. 'A great pity she's leaving Coriston. She's such an efficient, capable young woman.'

'Miss Darby's leaving too?' Thorne was interested at once. 'There's quite an exodus from the place. Do you happen to know why?'

It was Betty who answered. 'She's going to Australia. She's got a brother there. She'd have stayed at Coriston, but there's no chance of promotion. If only Mr Quarry would leave she could be our housemistress, but there's not much hope of that.'

Mrs Farrow, who seemed to be looking at her daughter in a new light, obviously surprised at Betty's knowledge of the inner workings of the school, glanced rather obviously at her watch and the Superintendent took the hint. 'Mrs Farrow, Miss Farrow, thank you both very much. You've been most helpful.'

He got to his feet and smiled at Betty. 'Incidentally, Miss Farrow, there must have been a lot of rumours going round Coriston last term. Did you ever hear anything about anonymous letters—people getting them, or sending them?'

'Anonymous letters?' Betty thought for a moment, then shook her head decisively. 'No, Superintendent.'

'Well, thanks anyway,' Thorne said. 'A very helpful little lady indeed,' he added to Abbot as he got into their car.

'Did you believe everything she said, sir?' Abbot asked.

'Not quite everything, no. She tends to dramatize. But she wasn't lying about that letter, Abbot. I don't think she sent it.' Thorne stroked his moustache thoughtfully. 'A good morning's work. Now we deserve a good lunch.'

CHAPTER 17

The Gales lived in a council house on the outskirts of
Reading. It had a small patch of sparse grass in front,
surrounded by a low fence to divide it from its neighbours.
Children playing in the street watched with interest as Abbot
drew up by the gate and the two detectives got out of the car.
It was obviously a neighbourhood that had seen better days,
but the Gales' house at least looked reasonably well cared
for, the curtains clean, the path free of debris.

The front door was opened to them by a woman of medium
height, broad-breasted, sallow of skin, with brown hair and
dark eyes. She bore no resemblance to the small, slight
Moira. 'Yes?' she said, regarding the two men with
suspicion.

'Mrs Gale?' Thorne said and, when she nodded, 'We're
police officers. We'd like a word with you about Moira.'

Mrs Gale's eyes widened in sudden fear. 'She's all right,
isn't she? Nothing—nothing else has happened?'

Thorne hastened to reassure her. 'But we do need a few
words, Mrs Gale. Perhaps it would be better if we came in.'

'Yes, I'm sorry. All this has been very upsetting. My poor
little Moira! You read about such things in the papers, but
you never think they'll happen to your own.'

Suddenly voluble, she ushered them into a small, gloomy
hall, and then into the front room on the right. Thorne
noticed the large colour television set, the video recorder, the
cassette player. They were all comparatively new and, he
guessed, all supplied on the instalment plan. The furniture
on the other hand looked old, the bit of carpet well-worn.
There was a big coloured photograph of Moira standing in
an ornate frame on the mantelshelf.

Thorne advanced towards it. 'A very pretty girl, your

daughter, Mrs Gale,' he said. 'We must ask you some questions about her.'

Mrs Gale seemed to detect some underlying menace in his words. 'It's not her that's done anything wrong,' she said. 'She's a good girl. All she did was try and get a lift, and there's no law against that. She works hard at school and she babysits, and she's got a part-time job at Mr Bronson's by the new shopping centre—as an assistant, like.' Mrs Gale was getting agitated. 'She's never been in no trouble with the police. You can ask at the school.'

'Mrs Gale, please don't get upset.' Thorne was soothing. 'We have to make these inquiries, you know. After all, the man she's accused also has an excellent reputation and he denies meaning her any harm.'

Moira's mother was scarcely listening. 'She could sell her story to the newspapers and make a lot of money. There were witnesses.'

'I should make her think carefully before she did anything like that, if I were you,' Thorne said.

Mrs Gale sniffed and almost tossed her head. 'Our neighbours say that even if the police don't charge him, we could take him to court for damages. But Moira doesn't want anything like that. She says the stories in the papers and on telly would be horrid for all of us, and anyway she's feeling sorry for the poor man, she says, though how she can be after what he did, I can't imagine.'

'Very generous of her,' Thorne said in an effort to stop the flow of words. He wasn't doing very well with Mrs Gale. He gave Abbot a nod, and the Sergeant took over.

'This was Moira's first visit to Colombury, wasn't it, Mrs Gale?' Abbot asked. 'She'd never been to see her auntie before?'

'No, and I wish she'd not suggested it now.'

'It was her suggestion? She wanted to go?'

'Yes. Why not?' Again, Mrs Gale seemed to take umbrage. 'She'd been working hard for her exams and she thought a few days away would do her good. It wouldn't cost much. She couldn't hope for another holiday like the one she had at Easter.'

'What was that?' Thorne asked as Abbot paused.

'It was one of those trips arranged by the school, or we wouldn't have let her go. Mr Kelsey—that's the head-master—took a party of them to Guernsey in the Channel Isles. Moira saved up for it specially. She pretended not to be excited about it, but she was. She'd never been across the sea before. I know she enjoyed it, though she didn't talk about it much afterwards.'

'Didn't she?' Abbot said. 'I should have thought she'd have been full of it.'

'I know. But she's a private sort of girl. She doesn't like to show her feelings much.'

'What does she do in her spare time, when she's not at school or at work?' asked Thorne. 'A lot of boyfriends?'

'She doesn't have much time for anything except school and the shop. Sometimes she goes to the disco. I tell her she works too hard, but she pays no attention.' Mrs Gale shook her head as if she didn't understand. She had quite lost her earlier unease, and was apparently prepared to discuss Moira at length. 'As for boys, it's the same. There's a nice lad next door but she won't look at him. She says she's in no hurry, and anyway she'd want something a lot better than him.'

'Very commendable,' Thorne said. 'Obviously a sensible girl. Ambitious, too. Eager to better herself.'

Whether it was his tone of voice or the actual words, Thorne wasn't sure, but it was quite obvious that once again he'd touched on some sensitive chord—some relic of a family quarrel, perhaps. Mrs Gale's sallow cheeks flushed, and she began to massage one thumb against the other in a nervous gesture.

'All young girls dream of marrying a prince and living in a palace,' she said defensively.

'Yes,' said Thorne. 'I suppose they do—even sensible ones.'

The Superintendent paused doubtfully. It was inevitable in such an inquiry that differing facets of an individual's character would become apparent, but the picture he was getting of Moira Gale seemed particularly confused. He would have liked to see her room; a lot could be learnt from someone's private place. But he decided against asking. He signalled to Abbot, stood up and bade Mrs Gale goodbye.

'Where to now, sir?' Abbot asked as the door of the council house shut firmly behind them and they walked down the short path to the gate. 'Kidlington? Colombury?'

Thorne shook his head. 'We've not finished here yet. Let's go and have a look at young Moira's shop. Find this new shopping centre. I think we passed it on the way to this estate. Remember?'

'Yes, sir. About a mile back.'

They had no difficulty in finding the shopping centre, but Mr Bronson's shop proved more elusive. Even after asking directions, they still drove past it twice. It was a small store in a narrow street, obviously just saved from demolition when ground was cleared for the new centre. Sandwiched between a cheap furniture store and a greengrocer, its window display was drab even by the surrounding standards.

'Not what you expected, eh, Abbot?' Thorne said.

'God, no. I'd have expected a dress shop, sir, or music perhaps, records and such like—something a young girl could go for.'

'So would I,' Thorne admitted, 'but our Moira's not your run of the mill sixteen-year-old, though that's not necessarily anything against her. I think I'll go in alone, Abbot. You find a phone. It's that Mr Kelsey we want to get hold of, the headmaster of a local school for kids of Moira's age. She said she was at a comprehensive, didn't she? It shouldn't be difficult to locate Kelsey. Try the local station if you have any trouble.'

Abbot went off and Thorne, having studied the window for a moment, entered Bronson's. It was a second-hand book-shop and, surprisingly in its location, obviously one of some quality. Most of the stock was concealed behind the glass-doored shelves that lined the walls, but some—obviously less valuable—was displayed on polished mahogany tables.

A man looked down with only mild interest as Superintendent Thorne came in. Alone in the shop, he was perched on a set of library steps, taking books from a shelf, inspecting them and rearranging them. He gave up the task with apparent reluctance; to Thorne it seemed that he much preferred it to serving customers.

'Can I help you?' he said as he climbed down the steps and came forward.

'Mr Bronson?'

'Yes. I'm Hector Bronson.'

The name suited him, Thorne thought. Mr Bronson was a small, rotund man, wearing a brown tweed suit, too thick for a warm summer's day, and hand-made shoes. Thorne noted the expensive watch, the signet ring, the silk tie, and decided that Hector Bronson probably didn't depend on the book business for his creature comforts.

'Mr Bronson, I was given your name as a referee for a Miss Moira Gale,' Thorne said, stretching the truth a little. 'I believe she's been working here as a part-time assistant. Has she been satisfactory?'

'Oh, more than satisfactory. Yes, indeed,' Bronson said at once. 'It's so hard to get young staff, especially in a shop like this. And we have a most extensive mail-order trade. We deal with customers all over the world. There are catalogues to be sent out, books to be packed—all that sort of thing. And some of the stock needs most careful handling.'

Bronson broke off as he saw Thorne glance outside, and laughed. 'Don't be put off by our location or our exterior, sir,' he said with some pride. 'The name of Bronson is very well known in the trade, and amongst bibliophiles. But Moira—

yes, she's a great help. About nine—ten months she's been coming here. Only after school and Saturdays and holidays, of course. She seems to like the work—and the books. I shall miss her. She's leaving school, is she? Applying for a full-time job?'

'It's not definite yet. She'd like to stay on at school for at least another year, but you know what it's like, Mr Bronson. A girl at home has to be fed and clothed and so on. There's pressure on the family, and if she could be earning—'

'Quite. Quite.' Bronson frowned. 'I'd have her here. As I say, she's very reliable, more than you can say for most youngsters these days. But there's really not enough work for more full-time staff. Now, if she could take a secretarial course—but I've another lady who comes in the mornings to deal with that sort of thing. Anyway, that's not the point, is it? She wants to stay on at school? You're from the Ministry of Education or something? Question of a grant, perhaps?'

'Something like that, Mr Bronson.' Thorne smiled. 'From what you say she's a splendid young person. Pity there aren't more like her. But, just for the record, you've never had any—any doubts about her at all?'

'No. No, none at all.'

But the Superintendent had noticed a momentary hesitation. It could mean nothing, he knew. Some people hated to commit themselves too positively. However, he decided to press the point.

'Money in the till never short at the end of the day?' he asked jovially and, as Bronson shook his head, remarking that they did little cash trade, 'No valuable books missing?'

Bronson answered indirectly. 'Books are always going missing in a bookshop. It's not surprising. They're lost if they're put on the shelves in the wrong place. They usually turn up again, of course.'

'Of course,' Thorne said, and waited.

'There was one book,' Bronson said at last. 'It was a George Orwell first edition, mint condition, with dust wrappers and a nice signed inscription. Worth quite a lot of money. I had an inquiry from an American collector not long before Easter, and I found the book missing. I could have sworn—' He stopped miserably. 'Naturally I asked Moira, but she knew nothing about it. She was very worried. I hoped we'd find the book, but we never did.'

'Would it be easy to dispose of, if it were stolen?' Thorne asked.

'Well, first of all you'd have to know it was valuable—and that limits the field. Then it would be useful to know your way around the trade. There might be some queries,' Bronson sighed, 'but there are plenty of dealers who'd give you a price for it without asking too many questions.'

'I understand,' Thorne said. 'Well, thank you for telling me about it, Mr Bronson. I don't imagine it's relevant, but one likes to know.'

'I'd hate you to think I'm accusing—'

'Of course not, Mr Bronson. I appreciate that,' Thorne said. 'And all that's been said is absolutely confidential. I know I can depend on your discretion.'

Thorne left the bookshop feeling very pleased with himself. He found Sergeant Abbot waiting in their car a little way along the street. Mr Kelsey had been located at home. On the phone he'd said he was working in his garden, but he'd be quite prepared to have a chat with them.

They learned little, however. He agreed that Moira Gale worked hard, was a good student and kept out of trouble, as far as he knew. But he admitted somewhat ruefully that in a big comprehensive school it was hard to keep track of everyone. The best that could be said was that Moira wasn't the sort of pupil who came to his attention very often.

'But I did get to know her a bit when I took a party to Guernsey at Easter,' he added. 'She struck me then as a reserved child, inclined to go off on her own. Yet she was terribly keen to come. Her class teacher told me the family

may have had a little difficulty in raising the money, but
Moira had a part-time job and did some babysitting, and
saved up hard to help. That shows something, surely—
determination, if nothing else.'

'Yes,' said Thorne, wondering if that was all it showed.

CHAPTER 18

The next day Superintendent Thorne and Sergeant Abbot
returned to Colombury and went directly to the cottage
where Moira Gale was staying with her aunt. This time it
was Moira who opened the door to them and it was obvious
from her wide-eyed stare that she'd had no warning of their
coming. For once they seemed to have succeeded in circum-
venting the grapevine that operated so well in the town.

This morning Moira was wearing a blue shirt and jeans,
and she'd done something to her eyes so that the injury to one
was hardly noticeable. Her hair was loose and two or three of
her shirt buttons were open, so that the gleam of a heavy gold
necklet was readily visible. Instinctively her hand rose, but
whether her first thought was to conceal the necklet or button
her shirt, Thorne had no way of telling. Somehow—it might
have been because of her unwelcoming expression or because
of the make-up on her eyes—she looked older than when
they'd last met her.

'Good morning,' Thorne said. 'May we come in?'

Moira made no direct reply. Instead, she called, 'Auntie,
it's the police again.'

Edna Gale came bustling from the rear of the cottage,
wiping her hands on her apron. She looked, if anything, less
pleased than her niece to see the two officers, and she didn't
bother to greet them. She said with some asperity, 'And what
do you want now? More questions, I suppose. I had my
brother-in-law on the phone last night from Reading. You've

been making Moira's mother sick with all your questions, worrying her to death. Anyone would think it was Moira who'd done wrong, not that Roystone man.'

'I've been questioning Mr Roystone too, Mrs Gale, I assure you,' Thorne said evenly. 'And I'm very sorry to bother you. I won't keep you and Moira long, but I hope you'll spare me a minute or two. May we come in?' he asked again.

'A fat lot of choice the likes of us have got,' Mrs Gale muttered, but she took off her apron, hung it on a peg in the passage and showed them into the front room. She didn't offer them seats and the quartet stood in an awkward group in the middle of the carpet.

'Mrs Gale, it's really you that we came to see, not Moira,' Thorne said. 'I know you've only returned here compara- tively recently, but you are a local woman. Do you know any people called Hilman?'

'Hilman?' Mrs Gale looked blank. 'No, I don't think so. Why?'

'What about Pierson or Grey?'

'There's a Tom Pearson that works at the garage—'

'No, I doubt if that'd be him, Mrs Gale,' Thorne inter- rupted. 'What about Steve Leyton? Ever heard that name?'

'No,' she said. 'Who are all these men? Why ask me about them?'

'Just one or two more,' said Thorne. 'John Quarry? What about him?'

'No,' Edna Gale said firmly. Then she frowned. 'Wait a minute, though. Isn't he one of the teachers at Coriston?'

'Yes, that's right,' Thorne smiled encouragingly and turned to Moira. 'Did any of those names mean anything to you, Moira?'

The girl shook her head. 'There are some Greys at my school, and a Pearson, I think, but they're not particular friends of mine and anyway they're in Reading. Why are you—'

Thorne ignored her implied question. 'Now, what about the Mortons?' he asked cheerfully. 'I'm sure Mrs Gale will know of them, even if you don't, Moira.'

'You mean Frank and Kate Morton? Billy's parents—the little boy Mrs Roystone killed. Of course I know them.' Mrs Gale was almost triumphant, as if she had at last scored a point. 'I was at the old elementary school just across the green with Frank Morton, though he's younger than me. I've known the family for years—all my life.'

'Then you can tell me where they live,' Thorne said, seemingly equally triumphant. 'Something's come up about that accident—an insurance matter—and I thought I might just be able to sort it out while I'm here in Colombury.'

Mrs Gale nodded her understanding, as if it were usual for detective-superintendents to make casual inquiries about insurance matters, or have difficulty in tracing the address of a couple whose child had been killed in a recent road accident. Her earlier hostility now seemed forgotten.

'I certainly can,' she said, and seemed about to ask them to sit down in the hope of a continuation of the conversation. But Thorne was already saying their goodbyes. Followed by Abbot, he went with Edna Gale to the front gate, where she directed them to the Mortons' house.

As they walked back to their car, Thorne said, 'Well, Abbot, did you get anything?'

'Not much, sir.'

Sergeant Abbot's instructions about the interview they'd just completed had been clear. He was to leave the talking to the Superintendent and to concentrate all his attention on Moira. Thorne would want to know later if she so much as blinked.

'She was very tense the whole time, sir. She stood still, too still, staring at you. I'm sure it wasn't natural. I got the impression she was expecting you to ask some awkward question that never materialized.'

'Pity!' Thorne snorted. 'If only I'd known what it was I'd
have asked it like a shot!'

Abbot grinned. 'As far as I could tell she didn't react to
any of the names you threw out, sir, except for Quarry, and
I'm not absolutely certain of that. It was a bit odd, as if she
didn't quite take in the name Quarry till her auntie mentioned Coriston, if you see what I mean. But she certainly
relaxed when you got on to the Mortons.'

Thorne sighed. 'Ah well. It was worth a try. Did you notice
her gold necklet, Abbot?'

'Yes, I did, sir, but—lots of people wear them these days,
men and women. In fact—'

'In fact, you've got one yourself? Don't let me catch you
wearing it on duty, Sergeant.'

'No, sir! I wouldn't dream of it. All I meant was, there's
nothing unusual about Moira having one.'

'You may be right,' Thorne said. They had reached the car
and he got in, did up his seat-belt and waited for Abbot to
start the engine before he continued. 'But you may be wrong.
We know Moira has no spare money. She had difficulty
raising enough for that Easter trip. Yet now she's got a fine
gold necklet that looked quite new to me.'

'These things can be pretty cheap, you know, sir,' protested Abbot. 'They don't have to be eighteen carat gold.
Perhaps her auntie bought it for her.'

'It's hard to tell,' said Thorne, 'but I've got a feeling the
one that girl was wearing was pretty heavy and good—and
expensive. I've just given Mrs Thorne something very like it
for her birthday, and I can tell you it set me back a bit.'

Abbot was silent for a moment. Then he said, 'Maybe Mr
Bronson had better do some stocktaking. More books may be
missing.'

Thorne grunted. His thoughts were on the Chief Constable, to whom he was expected to report that evening. He
didn't think the Chief Constable was going to like what he
had to say. He didn't much like it himself, but no one could

make bricks without straw. And straw was something of which there was certainly a shortage.

Thorne used the same maxim later in the day as he sat across the desk from his Chief Constable. 'It's unsatisfactory, sir, I know, but in my view what it really amounts to is that it's Mr Roystone's word against Moira Gale's.'

'And you don't altogether trust the girl?' The Chief Constable was a heavily built man, lethargic in body, but far from lethargic in mind.

Thorne shrugged. 'A personal opinion, sir. I've nothing positive against her, as I said. Everyone agrees she's a sensible girl, hard working, a good student. Never been in any kind of trouble. We could follow up that business of the missing book, but I doubt it would get us anywhere. Even if we could prove she nicked it, any lawyer worth his salt would turn it into a good sob story. Poor little girl, deprived, all her mates going on that holiday, and so on.'

'And anyway it's not relevant to the accusation. Even if it were admissible, it wouldn't necessarily do Roystone any good.'

'Probably the reverse, sir. The media would pulverize him,' Thorne said. 'Put Moira and Mr Roystone side by side and there's only one conclusion everyone will come to. Her great asset's her looks—she's small and dainty, long fair hair, blue eyes, and doesn't look her age. Butter wouldn't melt, and all that. From Roystone's point of view it's an awful pity she doesn't look more like a tart. Then Mr Roystone's story—that she attacked him—would be perfectly credible. But as things are, no. Certainly not with a jury.'

The Chief Constable looked at the ceiling above his desk. 'And the evidence?'

'There's her word against his, as I say. The witnesses—the Ingles—only saw the couple struggling on the ground, and that was from a moving car. But still, they did see a struggle, and the girl's clothes were torn. And there's this business of

Roystone's trousers being open. And the Farrow girl's story; that could be made to look pretty black. Sir, on balance, I think Roystone's only real defence, if it came to court, would be to show conspiracy—that someone had a grudge and put Moira up to it.'

'It would need to be quite a grudge, Thorne.'

'It would indeed, sir, though of course people brood and imagine that injuries or slights are worse than was really the case. But I've checked on nearly all the possibilities. I've not contacted Steve Leyton—his family say he's abroad. I haven't seen the Hilmans either, though their local police say it's true that Mr Hilman never leaves his property and they live a very isolated existence. It seems unlikely they'd have had the means or the opportunity to organize anything like this. As for the rest—though there could always be others I don't know about—I've not found a connection between any of them and Moira Gale, except for the Mortons. And that's pretty remote, through Moira's aunt.'

The Chief Constable was still staring at his ceiling. 'I suppose you could say the Mortons had a reason to hate the Roystones.'

'I'm sure they don't—hate the Roystones, I mean. I interviewed them at length, and I refuse to believe they're brilliant actors.' Thorne was emphatic. 'She broke down and cried when she was talking about her son, and he very nearly did too, but neither of them blame Mrs Roystone. The only critical thing either of them said was that she might have stopped fractionally sooner if she'd been used to driving that minibus.'

The Chief Constable nodded. 'They may have a point,' he said. 'I was sorry for them when I heard about the case at the time,' he added sympathetically. 'But it was just one of those things.'

'Mr Roystone's been extraordinarily good to the Mortons, you know, sir. Without having any formal obligation he's made a financial arrangement so that when Greg, their elder boy, gets to the right age he'll be able to go to Coriston with everything paid.'

'Has he now? That's pretty generous.'

'And Roystone made the Mortons swear never to tell anyone about the arrangement. Mrs Morton let it slip by accident. So I hope you won't know, sir.'

The Chief Constable nodded again. 'It's damnable,' he said. 'These cases are hell. Hugh Roystone's a nice man, and this could ruin him. I suppose it's possible he had a moment's madness, but—'

'It's possible, sir, I agree.' Thorne waited, but the Chief Constable didn't comment further and he continued. 'Anyway, I'm doubtful about a police prosecution. As you know, sir, these cases are notoriously difficult and in this one there seems a real possibility of a miscarriage of justice if we proceed. I suggest that at least we wait and see what the Gales do. I don't believe they'll bring a case. Certainly Moira seems to be all against it.'

'Why should she be opposed, one wonders. Her story would be worth something in the tabloids afterwards. As it is, she gains nothing from all this, does she?'

'It would seem not, sir.'

Superintendent Thorne had his own theory, but it wasn't one he was prepared to share with his Chief Constable. It was too far-fetched and had too many loopholes. To prove it would need a lot more man-hours of police time, a lot more public money—and he could still be wrong in the end. Probably better to let the matter rest where it was for the moment, and see if there were any developments.

The Chief Constable solved Thorne's dilemma for him. 'Let's sleep on it,' he said. 'But I expect you're right.'

'Fine, sir,' said Thorne. Strangely, he was relieved.

CHAPTER 19

Shortly after nine the following morning Hugh Roystone was having breakfast in the kitchen of his apartment. He had cooked himself an egg and some bacon, and forced himself to eat a little. But in the end he had given up, and sat staring at his plate as the bacon cooled and the egg congealed. It was reasonable, he thought, that his main feeling these days was of loneliness. It was something he'd never experienced before he married. But things had been very different then. Angrily he rejected the half-formed idea that in some ways they'd been better.

He was pushing his plate away from him when the phone rang. He got up quickly and hurried into the sitting-room. These days he invariably found himself grabbing the receiver as soon as possible; there was always the chance the call might be from Sylvia, announcing her decision to return to Coriston, and to him. So far all he had received from her were two postcards, mailed in London, each with the briefest of meaningless sentences.

'Mr Roystone?'

It was a woman's voice, he was certain, but either it was oddly muffled, or the line was bad. It certainly wasn't Sylvia. But suddenly he was afraid it was a message from her or about her, to say she was ill or had had an accident.

'Yes. This is Hugh Roystone,' he said sharply. 'Who's that?'

'It doesn't matter,' the voice said, and went on so quickly that he had difficulty in distinguishing the words. 'You know St Mary's church just outside Colombury. There's a farm track that comes out on the road beyond the rectory. If you want to learn something to your advantage about Moira Gale, be there. Come down the track. Noon today. And whatever you do keep the police out of it. We'll know, and you won't get anything.'

'Where? Who's that?' The questions were instinctive, but the line was already dead. Roystone replaced the receiver and went slowly back to the kitchen. He sat once more before his plate, staring into space.

In a few moments, he made an effort to pull himself together. If nothing else, the phone call had distracted him. Obviously he must keep the rendezvous. The message might be a hoax, but it could represent an opportunity to learn something. In spite of what the woman had said, he supposed he should really consult the police, but any heavy-handed intervention might reduce the chances of a useful encounter. No. He'd damn well go alone, but he'd be on his guard. And if he found that little bitch Moira Gale—or one of her friends—waiting for him with anything like blackmail on their minds, he'd—But what would he do? What could he do, he wondered, as he finally roused himself to clear the breakfast table.

'Who's that on the phone, Moira?' Mrs Gale called, as she bustled in through the back door of the cottage, clutching a large lettuce.

'No—no one,' Moira said.

'What do you mean, no one? I heard you talking. You can't have been talking to yourself, child. Besides, I heard the ping it always makes when you hang it up.' Edna Gale put the lettuce in the sink and came through the kitchen into the passage, where the telephone was on the wall. She found Moira leaning beside it, spots of heightened colour on her cheeks. 'What's the matter? Are you sick?'

'No. You startled me, that's all,' Moira said. 'I wasn't expecting you back so soon, Auntie. You said you were going to visit this lady who's ill and—'

'That only means popping through the hedge at the bottom of the garden and seeing how she is and if she wants any shopping done. It only takes a minute.' Mrs Gale looked hard at her niece. 'Moira, you were on the phone, weren't you? I did hear you talking.'

'What did you hear, Auntie?'

'I thought I heard you say "Mrs Roystone". Moira, what is this?'

Moira pushed herself away from the wall and went by her aunt into the kitchen. 'I'm sorry,' she said. 'I shouldn't have told you a fib, but I didn't want to worry you. It—it wasn't Mrs Roystone. It was Mr Roystone.'

'That man! What did he want? He can't have been after you again. Not now, with the police involved and all.'

'No, it wasn't like that, Auntie. He was sort of threatening me. He said if I didn't keep my mouth shut and go home he'd—he'd take me to court for the things I've been saying about him, and he'd win because he could afford the best lawyers, and he'd get enormous damages and ruin us all and—'

'The nerve of the man!' Mrs Gale said. She sat down heavily on a kitchen chair and eyed her niece. 'Moira, was this the first time, or has he phoned before and you've not told me?'

'Once.' Moira was reluctant. 'Auntie, it was just that I didn't want to worry you.'

'We must tell the police. We'll phone Sergeant Court.'

'No! No!' Moira said at once. 'I don't want any more to do with the police. It wouldn't do any good, anyway. He'd only deny it, or say I phoned him.'

'Well, if that's what you want,' Mrs Gale said doubtfully. 'But it's a shame, a crying shame. That's what it is. Here you are, meant to be having a nice holiday with me, and there's all this fuss and you never go out of the house or garden. You'll be wanting to go home soon too, I suppose.'

'Soon, Auntie, yes. I'll have to go. There's my job at the bookshop and Mum needs my help, you know. But I'll come again.' Moira leant forward and gave her aunt a warm hug.

'You've been so kind.'

'Nonsense.' Edna Gale was touched. Her two sons had emigrated to Canada and, though she'd approved of their decision, she still missed them and envied her brother-in-law and his wife, with Moira still at home. 'I only wish you could have gone out, like, and enjoyed yourself more.'

'Cheer up! I've made a big decision. I'm going out this morning,' Moira said. 'My eye hardly shows any more, and you're right, I can't hide away here all the time.'

'You'll come shopping with me, then?' Mrs Gale was pleased.

'Not shopping, Auntie, not today. Not the first time. I'm sorry, but I'd have to talk to people if I went with you.' Moira smiled apologetically. 'I don't think I could face that yet. I'll just go for a walk by myself, in the back roads where I probably won't meet anyone.'

John and Helen Quarry had intended to spend the day in London, shopping and lunching with their daughter, but at the last moment John cried off, pleading a stuffy nose and a sore throat. He drove Helen to the station, bought himself some lozenges at the chemist's in Colombury and returned to Coriston.

Back in his flat, he was restless. He read the newspapers, started to write a letter and abandoned the effort, and finally went downstairs intending to get some fresh air by strolling through the school grounds. Passing College House he was surprised to see a car he recognized as Frances Bell's outside the front door. Then Frances herself appeared.

'Hello,' Quarry said. 'What are you doing here? I thought you'd gone to stay with your sister.'

'I have. I mean, I am staying with her.' Frances looked a little embarrassed. 'Actually she was busy today with preparations for some church fête—not my kind of thing at all. I was clearly going to be under foot, so I thought I'd drive over to Oxford for lunch and call in on Paula Darby on the way.

I've got a book of hers and I wanted to give it back before she
went off to Australia.'

'And how's Paula?'

'Fine. Highly organized, as you'd expect. She didn't even
want the book back, because she was all packed and had
nowhere to put it. She was busy cleaning the cottage for the
new owners, though it looked pretty clean to me.' Frances
shrugged. 'Anyway, she obviously wanted to be rid of me and
get on with it, so I thought I'd come on here and look through
the mail and pick up my own.' Frances waved the two letters
she was carrying. 'Nothing very exciting, I'm afraid,' she
added.

'Have you seen Hugh?'

'No, he wasn't around.' Frances glanced at her watch. 'I
must be off. I'm going to Oxford. Goodbye for now, John.
Love to Helen.'

Quarry opened her car door for her. 'Goodbye, Frances.
Take care.' He watched her drive off. Then, suddenly
purposeful, he strode back to his house.

Time was a strange phenomenon, he thought unorig-
inally. First it crawled, and you had no idea what to do with
it. The next moment it had taken you unawares, and was
galloping away. Thrusting another lozenge in his mouth, he
made for his own car.

Moira had waited only till her aunt had left the cottage
before setting out herself. She knew she had quite a long walk
ahead of her and she wanted to allow plenty of time, so that
she didn't have to hurry. And, since she didn't intend to go
by the most direct route—through the centre of the town—
there was always a possibility she might get lost. But she
knew she had a very good sense of direction, and there was
sure to be someone around from whom she could ask the
way.

It was a warm and rather sultry day, and Moira didn't
particularly enjoy the walk. She was wearing a shapeless dress

that her mother had made for her. It was a shade of green she didn't like, and in the heat the synthetic material seemed to stick to her thighs, hampering her movements. But she plodded on, thinking how much pleasanter it was to walk on town pavements than through country lanes. Anyway, soon, in a day or two, she'd be able to leave this silly little place and get home to a real city. Inquiries from passers-by proved unnecessary, though she met two or three people, a local man walking his dog and a couple of hikers. In accordance with country custom, they said good morning politely as they passed, but otherwise took no interest in her.

Moira knew that the main road leading northwards out of Colombury divided into two on the outskirts of the town, and that the old church she was seeking was on the right-hand fork. Eventually she found that she had judged her way perfectly, for a lane led her on to this road almost opposite the church. In fact, she had chosen her route so well that she was early. To fill in a few minutes she crossed the road and went into the church, but it was surprisingly cold within the thick stone walls, and she came out shivering. For a while she sat in the sun on the churchyard wall. Then it was time.

She walked up the road, away from the town, past a modern house that seemed to be the rectory; at least, a path led directly to it from the church. A couple of cars went by, and a young girl on horseback. The track she was looking for was a turning to the left, but it was further along the road than she had expected, and she now found she had to hurry.

The track, when she turned into it, was narrow, just wide enough for a tractor and farm cart. Trees met overhead. There was plenty of shade, but the atmosphere in the shadow was oppressive. Moira walked as quickly as she could on the rather uneven earth, sweating a little, excited. After about fifty yards, she stopped. To her left was a gate into a field, and a little further on the stump of an elm tree that had been cut down. Ahead the lane took a sharp curve. This was clearly the place.

She had reached the tree-stump when another figure rounded the corner ahead. She recognized it, and felt a flash of triumph. She was on her way at last; anything was possible now. Smiling, she stood in the middle of the lane and waited.

A voice said, 'Hello, Moira.'

'Hello,' Moira said. 'I'm glad you've come. Have you brought my money?'

There was no reply. All Moira saw were two hands reaching for her neck. It was only seconds before she blacked out.

Half an hour later, at noon precisely, Hugh Roystone found Moira Gale's body. The bruises on her neck, and her cyanosed lips and cheeks told their story only too clearly. Roystone thought of an attempt at resuscitation, but he knew from the moment he touched her cold skin that it would be useless. Then the ambiguity of his own position passed through his mind like a shock-wave. Of course, it was a trap. He had made no attempt to conceal his car, merely parking it on the main road by the rectory. And he had made no attempt to conceal his movements. He stood up and looked round almost furtively, fully expecting to see Thorne or Abbot rising from the undergrowth, responding to a tip-off. And even if that was implausible, there was no doubt that he must be a prime suspect. The best—the only—thing he could do was make away as quietly as possible, and hope.

It was not till early afternoon that a party of children from the local pony club came along the track to where Moira Gale lay. Rain in the interval had made its surface soft, and the ponies' hooves effectively destroyed any evidence there might have been in the ground.

CHAPTER 20

The pony club leader, a sensible woman in her early twenties, hastily herded her young charges back along the track away from the appalling sight. As soon as she reached the further road, she hurried to the nearest house and phoned the local police. Sergeant Court and a constable were on the scene within minutes and, as soon as he recognized Moira Gale, the Sergeant was in touch with Kidlington. By the time Superintendent Thorne and Sergeant Abbot arrived, the track had been closed at either end and officers posted to protect the surrounding area.

Thorne and Abbot left their car by the rectory, and picked their way carefully towards the body. They found the police surgeon, Dr Band, still examining it. As they approached he got to his feet.

'I know what you're going to ask,' he said without preamble, 'and I'll tell you what I think. She's been dead some hours—since around noon, say—and you've only got to look at her to see there's no question of an accident. Manual strangulation, for a cert—and by someone who knew what he was doing.'

Thorne nodded. He showed no surprise at the doctor's remarks. He just stood and looked down at Moira's body, his expression grim.

'Molested?' he said sharply.

'No. No suggestion of that.' Band bent down and carefully pulled aside the neck of Moira's dress. 'She's not been robbed either. Her watch is a cheap affair, but that gold necklet's worth a bit.'

'Between fifty and a hundred quid,' Thorne said. The doctor looked at him curiously, but the Superintendent made no attempt to explain. He hadn't liked Moira Gale. He liked

her no more now that she was dead. But he blamed himself.
Whatever his feelings towards her he should have forseen
this possibility. He sighed. 'Poor little bitch!' he said almost
under his breath.

He turned to his Sergeant. 'Well, Abbot, at first I thought
it was a bit *infra dig* to involve the Serious Crimes Squad with
Moira Gale. It seems I was wrong. We've a murder on our
hands. Get with it, man—the works—right away!' He looked
at the trees surrounding them and meeting overhead. 'We'll
need a lot of men to search this lot, and we'd better have an
incident van as soon as possible. And wait for me in the
car,' he added as the Sergeant hurried off to radio for immediate support. As Thorne turned back Sergeant Court
and one of his constables were covering the body. Dr
Band was preparing to depart. 'Okay?' he said. 'It's
all yours now. The pathologist'll know where to find me
if—'

'Fair enough, Doctor,' said Thorne. 'You'll let me have a
report as soon as—'

'I know. By yesterday. I'll do my best.' The doctor hurried
away.

'Now, Sergeant,' Thorne said to Court. 'In the meantime,
you've got the woman who found her—with all those
damned horses?' He looked morosely back along the track at
the churned-up ground.

'Well, no, sir. She had to take her class—they were only
kids—back to the stables, but she's well-known around here.
We can see her any time you like, sir.'

'Later,' said Thorne. 'I doubt if she can tell us much. Have
you got enough men to keep some on duty here till the mob
arrives? They can start a preliminary search. And what we
need's a bit of local house to house right away, before people
start to forget. Did anyone see Moira this morning? Was
anyone on this track? Any cars parked around? You know the
sort of thing. Your people can do it as well as we can, if not
better.'

'Yes, sir. I'll get on to it.'

'Mrs Gale, Edna Gale, the aunt, she's not been told yet, I hope?'

'No, sir. But—'

'But what?'

'Actually Edna Gale phoned the station earlier this afternoon. She was worried about Moira. She said the girl had gone for a walk and not come back for her midday dinner. I told her Moira had probably got lost or something, and not to worry yet awhile. And when I heard about the body I wanted to make sure before—'

'I see,' said Thorne thoughtfully. 'Anyway, that's fine. Now what I want is one of your WPCs to meet me at Mrs Gale's in—say—ten minutes. Plain clothes preferably, and she's not to go in till Abbot and I get there. Can you lay that on?'

'Of course, sir. I'll call from my own car right away, sir,' said Sergeant Court.

Thorne and Abbot set off for Edna Gale's cottage a few minutes later. They drove in silence. Thorne, slumped in his seat, eyes closed, head on his chest, might have been asleep, but Abbot knew better. He wasn't in the least surprised when, as soon as they reached their destination, the Superintendent sat up, smoothed his moustache and looked purposeful. By now, he thought, he ought to be used to George Thorne's little ways.

But Thorne, if he didn't surprise the Sergeant as much as when they had first worked together, could still puzzle him. Suddenly he said, 'There's a connection somewhere, Abbot, and we've missed it—unless I'm quite wrong. I suppose that's always possible.'

'Yes, sir.' Thorne glanced up sharply. 'I meant about the—the connection—as you say, sir,' Abbot added hastily.

A girl in a summer dress, breathless from hurrying, knocked on the car window, and introduced herself as WPC

Green. Thorne nodded brusquely as he heaved himself out of the door.

'You know the set-up?' he asked.

'Yes, sir. I know Mrs Gale and I've even met little Moira. I came with Sergeant Court to see her after the assault.'

'Good. Give the woman plenty of tea and comfort. But keep her away from the phone, if you can. Try and avoid any local calls; we don't want stories spreading too quickly. Understand?'

Without waiting for an answer Thorne led the way up the path to the cottage. He had no time to knock before the door was opened and an anxious-faced Mrs Gale was staring at them in apprehension.

'Moira!' she said at once. 'Something's happened to poor little Moira. I knew it. When she didn't come home for her dinner I knew something awful had happened.'

'Mrs Gale, please—' Thorne wasn't at his best on such occasions, and he was happy to let WPC Green take over.

The girl led Mrs Gale into the front room and told her of Moira's death as simply as she could. Mrs Gale wept. Abbot went to put on the kettle, and Thorne stared out of the window trying to conceal his impatience. He was glad when Mrs Gale's tears began to subside, and he felt able to speak. Her immediate response was predictable.

'Questions! Questions! That's all the police ever do—ask questions,' she said through her sobs. 'If you'd arrested that Mr Roystone when he first attacked her he wouldn't have had a second chance, and my Moira would still be alive.'

WPC Green was shocked. In spite of the presence of a detective-superintendent from Kidlington and his sergeant, she spoke instinctively, 'Mrs Gale, you mustn't say such things!' she protested. 'You can't say Mr Roystone did it, just like that, without any real evidence.'

But Thorne wasn't entirely surprised at Mrs Gale's accusation and he intervened. 'Mrs Gale, why blame Mr Roystone? Have you any reason? Or was it only because—'

'Because he threatened her, that's why! I ought never to have let her go out by herself, not after what he said to her, but she was worried about people seeing her poor eye and—' Edna Gale broke down and sobbed, and Thorne had to wait until she had again recovered herself.

Finally she sipped some tea, and went on. 'I should have told the police before, but Moira didn't want me to. She said it would only cause more trouble and he'd only deny it. He phoned her here at least twice, and said if she didn't stop spreading stories about him she'd regret it and we'd all be sorry. Oh, I can't remember the exact words, but that's what it meant.'

'These phone calls, Mrs Gale? When were they? Are you sure it was Mr Roystone? Did you speak to him yourself?'

Edna Gale shook her head. 'No, but it was him all right. At first I thought I head Moira say Mrs Roystone, but she told me it was Mr Roystone.'

'And when was this, Mrs Gale?' repeated Thorne quite gently.

'The last time was just this morning. There was another time he phoned, but I don't exactly know when. Moira didn't tell me about it till today. She said she didn't want to worry me. Poor dear child!'

Mrs Gale sobbed again for a moment and then recovered herself once more. When she spoke, her voice was stronger. 'Look, Superintendent, Moira never gossiped—about the Roystone business, I mean. It was the Ingles—the butchers. I know they saved her, but it was them that talked about it. Moira never said a word, except to the police. She's hardly been out of the house to talk to anyone. But that man—that Mr Roystone—he blamed her. It's not fair.' She raised her head from her sodden handkerchief. 'But nothing's fair, is it?'

'It depends what you mean by fair, Mrs Gale,' Thorne said neutrally. 'I assure you we'll inquire into everything you've said. Is there anything else you can tell us that might help?' Edna Gale shook her head. 'No? All right then. Miss

Green's going to stay with you. She'll get a doctor if you think you need one. We'll be off, but first I'd like to have a look at Moira's room. You won't mind?'

'No. It's the door facing you at the top of the stairs,' Mrs Gale said absently. 'But what about Bert and Meg?' she exclaimed suddenly. 'I must phone them.'

'Bert and Meg? Oh, her parents,' said Thorne. 'That's all being taken care of. Leave it to us for the moment and call them later, or maybe they'll phone you. I expect they'll want to come up here to look after—look after things,' he finished rather lamely.

With a nod to WPC Green, the Superintendent made his escape and, together with Abbot, inspected the bedroom that Moira had occupied. It yielded little of interest. All Moira seemed to have brought with her on her visit were a few inexpensive clothes and Lytton Strachey's biography of Queen Victoria, borrowed from the Reading public library.

'Serious reading for a girl on holiday, don't you think, Abbot, even if she did work in a bookshop?' Thorne said. 'I'd have expected a romantic novel or the story of some pop star. But I suppose it could be a set book, though she's just taken her O-levels.'

'Perhaps it was some kind of holiday task, sir.'

'Maybe.' Thorne sighed. 'And maybe we'll have to find out.'

Abbot stared at his superior officer in surprise.

Hugh Roystone himself opened the door of his apartment to them. He was wearing khaki shorts and a shirt open to the waist, revealing a strong, hairy chest. His eyes were bright, his face alive with happiness. But the brightness faded at the sight of the two detectives, and his expression became at first agitated, then resigned.

'Oh Lord, it's you again,' he said rather hesitantly. 'Well, I suppose you'd better come in, though it's not the most convenient time.' He waved them ahead of him into the sitting-room and indicated the fair young woman in a blue linen dress who had risen from the sofa. 'My wife, Sylvia. Darling, this is Superintendent—Detective-Superintendent—Thorne and Sergeant Abbot. I was telling you about them; they're from the Thames Valley Police.'

'How do you do?' The flush in Sylvia Roystone's cheeks deepened. She looked startled, almost frightened. She didn't offer her hand.

Thorne bowed. He had noted the two glasses, half full, on the long, low table in front of the sofa and the bottle of champagne on a tray. 'I'm sorry,' he said. 'We seem to have interrupted a celebration.'

'It can wait,' Roystone said. 'I'd offer you both a glass, but I'm sure you're on duty. This isn't a social call, I take it.'

'No, sir, it's not.' Thorne took the seat towards which Roystone motioned. 'Thank you.' He looked inquiringly at Sylvia. 'You said you'd mentioned us to your wife, so I imagine she's fully in the—'

'—in the picture about Moira Gale,' Roystone interrupted. 'Yes, now she is. You can ask your questions in front of her.'

Sylvia Roystone had returned to her place on the sofa again, but Roystone remained standing. Now he began to pace up and down. Thorne watched him for a moment without speaking. Abbot had found himself an upright chair to one side of the room, and was unobtrusively taking out a notebook.

Thorne said, 'There *are* one or two more questions, I'm afraid, sir. First, would you mind telling me what you've been doing today.'

'Today?' Roystone stopped his pacing and turned away, seemingly unsurprised at the question. 'Damn all, really. I—I went for a drive this morning and had lunch in a pub.'

'Which pub, sir? And what route did you take?'

There was a pause before Roystone continued in a mono-tone, 'I was restless. I drove into Colombury, filled up with

petrol at that big new garage on the far side of the town from
here, and made a circle back. I stopped at the Wheatsheaf for
a pint and a bite to eat. And I assure you I didn't pick up any
hitch-hikers.'

'You were driving your Mercedes?'

'Yes.'

Thorne turned to Sylvia. 'You drove here, Mrs Roystone?
From London? You've been looking after a sick friend, I
understand.'

'No. I mean yes. I—' Sylvia was clearly flustered.

'Superintendent! I'll answer any questions you like about
myself, however damned stupid they are. But I won't permit
you to intimidate my wife.' Roystone was angry. 'What's the
point of all this, anyway?'

'Moira Gale has received some threatening telephone
calls, sir. We need to trace the caller.'

'And that takes a detective-superintendent and a sergeant.
My God! No wonder the police are short of manpower.'
Roystone's mood had changed, and he put down his champagne glass and poured a measure of neat whisky. He said,
'Superintendent, if you'll believe me, maybe I can save you
some trouble. Never, never, never have I telephoned—or
written—to Moira Gale. Until that one unfortunate occasion, I'd never set eyes on her. And I wish to God I'd never
even heard the damned girl's name. Does that satisfy you?'

'Thank you, sir,' Thorne said mildly. He paused, then,
'What about you, Mrs Roystone? Your husband never gave
you time to answer my last questions.'

'Of course she's not phoned Moira Gale! It wasn't till this
morning that—'

'Please, sir! Let Mrs Roystone speak for herself.'

'It's all right, Hugh. That's not what the Superintendent
was asking. Superintendent, I don't see that it's any of your
business what I've been doing, but I don't mind telling you.
I've not been looking after a sick friend—that was an excuse
to prevent gossip in the school. I've been staying in a small

hotel in Kensington by myself. I'll give you the name and you can check. I wanted to think, that's all.' She hesitated and looked at her husband. 'It's not been easy, getting married and coming to Coriston where everyone except me seemed to belong and know everything and—Oh, what more can I say? Perhaps if it hadn't been for that ghastly accident—'

Sylvia stopped, her voice suddenly hoarse, and Roystone added more champagne to her glass and handed it to her. She sipped at it, then turned once more to Thorne. 'You know about Billy Morton, Superintendent?'

'Oh yes, Mrs Roystone. It was, as you say, ghastly—but an accident,' Thorne said. 'You shouldn't blame yourself.'

Surprised by his sympathy, Sylvia smiled suddenly. 'Anyway, the accident's got nothing to do with Moira Gale and her accusations. They're a separate horror I'd never heard of till this morning. I suppose there must have been something in the papers, but I missed it.'

'Not much, fortunately, and my name's not been mentioned,' Roystone said. 'Otherwise I could sue—if I were prepared to face the publicity. I may have to yet.'

'You knew nothing about the accusation against your husband until you got back to Coriston, Mrs Roystone?' Thorne asked.

'No, no. That's what brought me back. I met Helen Quarry—you must know John Quarry, he's Hugh's deputy—in Selfridges, quite by chance, and we had coffee together. She told me, so I caught the first train to Oxford and took a taxi from there. It cost the earth, but I didn't have my car. I've not driven since the accident. And I had to get here.' Sylvia Roystone drew a deep breath. 'I love my husband, Superintendent. I know he's a good man. I had to tell him I believed in him and knew all this was—was total nonsense.'

'Mrs Roystone, I'm sure your husband must be glad to hear that, and to have you with him.' Thorne got to his feet and addressed Hugh Roystone directly. 'Sir, things haven't

been easy for you recently, I know, and they're unlikely to get
better in the near future.'

'What do you mean by that?' said Roystone. Again his
mood had changed, this time to resignation.

'Mr Roystone, Mrs Roystone, there's something I must
tell you. Maybe I should have told you when I first arrived,
but I judged it best not to.' Superintendent Thorne spoke
slowly, weighting his words with importance. 'Moira Gale is
dead. She was murdered—strangled—this morning or early
afternoon on the farm track just north of St Mary's rectory on
the outskirts of Colombury.' Thorne turned to Roystone.
'Have you any comment, sir?'

There was a momentary hesitation, then Roystone said,
'It's all right, Superintendent. I know I'm not a very good
liar. Let me tell you. But first, understand clearly—I did *not*
kill Moira Gale. I was phoned about half past nine this
morning . . .'

Five minutes later, Hugh Roystone concluded, 'So that
was that. I'm not very proud of myself, but I suppose I
panicked. My only excuse is that there was nothing I could
do to help her.'

Detective-Superintendent Thorne seemed oddly unsurprised by Roystone's recital. 'You might have told us
about the phone call, sir,' was all he said.

'I've tried to explain why I didn't,' said Roystone. 'Who-
ever phoned took great care to warn me off. And I hoped
against hope that something useful would come out of some
kind of meeting—something to put an end to this awful
uncertainty. I didn't know if it was Moira on the phone, but
even if it was—or someone acting on her behalf—I thought I
could cope with an attempt at blackmail. Even another
attack might have proved something. But the last thing I
expected was to be faced with Moira's body.'

Again Thorne made no direct comment on Roystone's
story. To Sergeant Abbot's surprise, he merely said, 'If I
were you, I wouldn't mention any of this to anyone for the

moment, Mr Roystone.' And, as he turned to go, he added, 'I'll want your assurance that you won't be leaving Coriston or the Colombury area without informing me.'

It was at this point that Sylvia Roystone, sitting momentarily forgotten on the sofa, dropped her champagne glass, gave a small whimpering cry and keeled over sideways in a dead faint.

CHAPTER 21

It was late and dark by the time Thorne and Abbot reached Reading, and they were relieved to see lights still on both upstairs and down in the Gales' house. Thorne belched gently as, for the second time in three days, they walked up the short path and he put his finger on the bellpush by the front door; he had, perhaps unwisely, insisted on stopping for a hasty meal at a nearby café before tackling this tricky interview, but the food had been greasy and indigestible. He thought fleetingly of home and bed and Miranda, but he reminded himself that Bert and Meg Gale were suffering more extreme discomfort, mental if not physical.

'Yes? What is it?'

By the light of the street lamps they could see a face peering down at them through the door, held partly open by a chain. The face belonged to a tall man with brown eyes and dark hair beginning to recede, who looked tired, perhaps a little drunk. His words had been slightly slurred.

'Detective-Superintendent Thorne and Detective-Sergeant—'

But the chain was already being released and the door opened more widely. 'I know. The wife said you were here the other day. Come along in. I'm Bert Gale, Moira's dad.'

Unlike his wife, Bert Gale had no pretensions. He had been sitting in the kitchen, and that was where he took the two police officers. There was a plate of uneaten food beside the sink, a couple of dirty saucepans on the stove and some cans of beer on the table.

'I was trying to get tight,' he said simply. 'The wife's all right for the moment. She's asleep by now. She collapsed when we heard about Moira—that girl meant everything to her—but we got the doctor, and he gave her some kind of shot. The nurse is going to look in in the morning.'

'Fine,' said Thorne. He pulled up a chair and sat down, gesturing to Abbot to do the same.

'Help yourself,' Bert Gale said, and pushed some cans of beer towards them.

'Thanks.' To Abbot's surprise, Thorne accepted. 'Mr Gale, we're sorry to intrude on you at this time, but we've got our job to do.'

Bert Gale nodded. 'Sure. I guess I've been waiting for you. Your chaps who came to break the news said there was no doubt she was murdered, but they said it was quick.'

'I think that's true. I don't think she suffered.'

'But was she—was she raped this time? Was it the same chap? The one who—'

'There's no sign of anything like that, Mr Gale. And we're not sure who did it yet. That's why we're here. We want you to help us.'

'Anything I can tell you, I will. Anything that'll help find the bugger—'

'First, we need to know all we can about Moira, Mr Gale. Could we have a look at her room, for instance?'

'Sure,' Bert Gale said immediately. 'But you'll have to not make a noise. The wife's right next door, and I don't want her disturbed. Not yet.'

It was quite clear that Bert Gale had no wish to come with them, and Thorne led Abbot very quietly up the stairs. It was a small house and, even without Gale's brief directions and the sound of faint snoring from behind one upstairs door, Moira's room was obvious.

It was a young girl's room, with white-painted furniture, a blue rug on the floor, blue and white curtains and bedspread. It was a surprisingly pretty room, with a comfortable chair and a desk in one corner, and it looked as if Moira had spent a good deal of her time there. Over the bed was a photograph of Moira herself, a copy of the one they had seen in the front room downstairs on their previous visit. On the opposite wall hung a photograph of the Royal Family, cut from some magazine and carefully framed. Instead of the posters of pop stars that might have been expected in a teenager's room were two highly coloured travel agents' posters of Guernsey, one of the town of St Peter Port and the other of Castle Cornet. Thorne inspected the photographs and the posters, glancing from one to the other, his expression alive and questioning. Sergeant Abbot noticed the Superintendent's glances and frowned, but made no comment.

Without a word, the two detectives set to and searched the room. They were expert, thorough and made very little noise. Item by item, Moira's pathetic little secrets were revealed.

Thorne quickly found the key to the locked desk taped under its bottom drawer. Inside was a National Savings book. Moira had clearly been a careful saver; her account had mounted steadily during the past eighteen months or so, and now showed a balance of over three hundred and eighty pounds. Most of the credits were regular—her pay from the bookshop, no doubt—but five or six were largish and irregular. Thorne regarded these speculatively; one of them was probably the stolen Orwell, he thought—and the others? The credit of a hundred pounds a few weeks ago? The debits were easier to place—the payment for the trip to Guernsey earlier in the year, small withdrawals presumably for personal expenses, and one that could account for the gold necklet.

Thorne grimaced and turned to the remaining contents of the drawer. Among these were a scrap album and some loose photographs and articles cut from magazines and newspapers. Leafing through them with interest, he was interrupted by Abbot.

'Strange, sir,' the Sergeant said quietly, 'she must have had some hang-up on the Royals. Nearly all her books are about them.'

'Yes,' Thorne said, staring at a photograph Moira had stuck into the album next to one of her own. 'It looks as if she had delusions of grandeur. Anything else strike you?'

'Not really. There's a box with a few bits of costume jewellery. Only one thing looks a bit different. Here—it's a small silver medallion on a chain, with a coat of arms on one side and an outline map of Guernsey on the other. It looks as if it might be a bit more valuable, though not like that gold necklet she was wearing.'

The Superintendent nodded. 'Anything else?'

'She didn't go in for clothes much.' Abbot sounded puzzled. 'But there's one nice suit and a few pretty dresses. Funny she didn't take at least one of them to Colombury with her.'

'Perhaps she knew she wouldn't need them there,' Thorne said noncommittally. He put the savings book in his pocket and clutched the scrap book. 'Come on, Abbot, let's go and talk to Bert Gale again.' As they left the room the Superintendent took a last frowning look at the two pictures on the walls and the poster on the door.

Gale was where they had left him, sitting at the table, staring straight ahead. But he had pulled himself together to some extent, cleared away the empty beer cans and put on a kettle. Once again Thorne and Abbot took chairs opposite him.

Thorne said, 'Mr Gale, earlier you told us we could ask you anything. I've got one or two questions that are rather personal.' Thorne paused. 'Mr Gale, was Moira your daughter?'

Abbot looked up sharply in surprise, but Bert Gale

answered without hesitation, 'No, but we loved her as if she'd been our own. We've—we'd—had her ever since she was a small baby, adopted, all legal-like.' Bert Gale sighed. 'Meg had to have an operation soon after we were married, so she couldn't—'

'I understand,' said Thorne. 'Did Moira know she was adopted?'

'Yes. We told her. Actually she asked us. It was when she was about ten, I remember. Some busybody at her school had seen us and said we didn't look much like her. Nor we did. She was such a fair, delicate little thing.'

'Did she know who her real parents were?'

'No. We said no one knew. She'd—we said she'd been found in a basket at the hospital gate.'

There was another pause. Then Thorne said gently, 'And was that true, Mr Gale?'

Gale shook his head. 'No, it wasn't. But we wanted to put her off ever asking any more questions, even when she grew up. Oh, she'd been found all right, but in a public lavatory down by the docks. The authorities said her mother was probably a whore and her father a sailor off one of the boats. You couldn't tell a child that, could you?'

'So really she was able to imagine anything she liked,' Thorne said softly. 'Even that she might be related to the Royal Family?'

'Oh, that, yes.' The kettle had begun to sing and Gale got up to heat the teapot and make some tea. 'That was a sort of family joke at one time, though I'm not sure Meg didn't encourage it too much. An old girl down the road said Moira looked just like the present Queen when she was a little princess, and that started it. Meg used to call Moira her little princess. But that was ages ago. I'd forgotten all about it, and I'm sure Moira had.'

'I'm not so certain, Mr Gale. Have you seen this before?' The Superintendent pushed the scrap book across the kitchen table.

'No.' Gale shook his head. He looked bewildered.

'Or this?'

It was the National Savings book, and again Gale shook his head. He opened it slowly. 'I don't understand,' he said. 'She earned money all right, at that old bookshop and babysitting and we always let her keep it for herself. I suppose we spoilt her. But she never seemed to spend it much, except for that trip to Guernsey, and we helped her a bit with that. But this—nearly four hundred pounds—' Suddenly, as he glanced through the savings book, his expression changed. 'No! The little—'

'What is it, Mr Gale?'

'Nothing,' Bert Gale said roughly. 'It doesn't matter now. The tea'll be brewed. Want a cup?'

'Mr Gale, you'd better tell us what upset you just then,' Thorne said. 'It was something in the savings book?'

Bert Gale sighed. 'It doesn't matter now,' he repeated. 'She's dead. What does it matter what she did?'

'Mr Gale, please.' Thorne was losing patience.

Gale stabbed his finger at a credit entry in the savings book dated during the previous year. 'I can make a good guess where she got that from. It's my pay packet. I always thought she'd taken it, but she wept and wept and swore she hadn't till I believed her. I decided Meg must have been right and I'd lost it on the way home from the pub.'

Thorne stood up. 'We'll need to take these two books, Mr Gale. Sergeant Abbot'll give you a receipt.'

'Take what you like.' Bert Gale shook his head miserably. 'I don't understand. We were always kind to her. Meg went without things so she could have them. The big telly and the video. They were all for her sake. We did our best.'

'But their best wasn't good enough,' Thorne said, as he and Abbot drove back to Kidlington. 'I doubt if Moira really believed she'd ever be summoned to the Palace to take her rightful place with the Royals. But I'm pretty sure she fantasized she'd got royal blood somewhere. It made her determined to improve herself so that one day she'd be—be worthy of it, as it were.'

Abbot had little sympathy with his Superintendent's flight of imagination. 'All it did was make her a thief,' he said abruptly. 'That book was one thing, but poor old Bert's pay packet! It's a pity they didn't tell her about the sailor and the tart.'

Thorne was scarcely listening. 'She tried to get the best out of the education that was available to her, to improve her speech, to save. Even seizing the chance "to go abroad" would fit the pattern. That trip seems to have meant a good deal to her. Those better clothes, Abbot—they were probably for the great holiday.' Thorne lapsed into silence for a moment, then roused himself. 'Guernsey? I wonder if—' He stopped suddenly, as if half afraid to voice his thoughts.

The Sergeant looked at Thorne curiously. Then, to break the lengthening silence, he said, 'And what about that gold necklet, sir?'

'Perhaps she was tempted. Perhaps she had a windfall. Perhaps—' Thorne stopped again.

'A windfall? Do you mean another theft, sir?'

'Perhaps. Perhaps payment for services rendered, or to be rendered.'

Sergeant Abbot was no fool, or he wouldn't have been working with Thorne. He said, 'To trap Mr Roystone, say?'

'It's a thought, isn't it, Bill?' Thorne, having had his own idea partly played back to him, was now at his most affable. 'It fits, you know. "X" meets Moira, or already knows her. Moira looks the part and Moira'll do most things for money. "X" bribes her to accuse Roystone of assault. Then "X" gets afraid that Moira might get scared and come out with the truth, or Moira tries a little blackmail on the side, so "X" plans a killing. And a killing that throws suspicion on Roystone—perfect! All it needed was a simple phone call making sure he'd be on that track by the church at a certain

time. And we don't know yet if anyone saw him, or his car.
Maybe someone'll come forward, but even if they don't the
villain's lost nothing; Roystone's clearly a suspect. Either it's
something like that, or Roystone's lying through his teeth.'

'You don't believe that, sir. You think Roystone's
innocent.'

'Yes,' Thorne said decisively. 'I do. I can't believe he'd
have been so happy with his wife when we descended on him
this afternoon if he'd just deliberately strangled the girl.'

'And "X", sir?' Abbot said tentatively. 'You've some
idea?'

'Not really,' Thorne admitted. 'But if I were a betting man
I'd put my money on someone at Coriston. There's someone
there who hates Roystone's guts, and somewhere there's a
connection between that someone and Moira Gale. That
connection's what we've got to find, Abbot.'

CHAPTER 22

The paperwork inevitably associated with the investigation
of all major crime had started to come in, some of it by telex,
some in the form of computer print-out, but most picked out
with two fingers on a typewriter by the police officer directly
responsible for the individual inquiry.

Twelve hours after his return from Reading, Superintendent Thorne sat at his desk, studying the files that had
accumulated concerning what had come to be known—by
the police, at least—as the Roystone-Gale case. Sergeant
Abbot occasionally came into the office with fresh pieces of
information. Roystone-Gale, thought Thorne: it was a
simple way of referring to the events of the past few days
but, luckily for Hugh Roystone, the media hadn't yet dared
to be quite so explicit. Thorne sighed, and returned to the
files.

'Manual strangulation,' as Dick Band had said, was the gist of the pathologist's report. The neck bruising suggested the attack had been from the front, and every indication was that the victim had been conscious when the attack took place. There were no signs of a struggle and the attack was obviously totally unexpected. The assailant, who could be either male or female, was almost certainly known to the victim.

Moira's movements had been traced fairly readily. The man who had passed her while walking his dog recalled her. More importantly, the Reverend Simon Kent, the rector of St Mary's church, had seen her sitting on the churchyard wall at about twenty past eleven, as if, he said, she were waiting for someone. Or waiting for an appointment in the lane just five minutes away, Thorne thought. The rector had also noticed a Mercedes car parked in the road outside his home some half an hour later. That at least was a point in Roystone's favour, Thorne said to himself. No intending murderer in his senses would leave a distinctive car parked close to the likely scene of the crime.

The Superintendent pulled towards him a list, acquired from Hugh Roystone, of all the staff at Coriston, with their home addresses, and their addresses in term-time where these differed from their homes. A great deal of patient checking was taking place, and already it was known that John Quarry had not, in fact, gone to London yesterday with his wife; in spite of a bad sore throat, he had driven into Oxford. Frances Bell had indeed visited Paula Darby at her cottage, had gone on to Coriston, and also subsequently to Oxford. Mark Joyner and his wife had been back in their house at Coriston for three days after a brief holiday. There was a lot more, and most of it, Thorne knew, would prove to be quite irrelevant.

The intercom interrupted him. It was Abbot. 'Sir,' he said, 'it's Lord Penmereth. He's been on the phone to the Chief Constable, and the Chief wants you to speak to him.'

'Okay. Put him through,' Thorne answered resignedly.

Lord Penmereth had just read of Moira Gale's death, and had heard from Hugh Roystone of the circumstances. He wanted to know from Thorne personally what was being done, and how Coriston might be affected. Thorne was purposely vague, but he gave what information he thought advisable, and promised that he would do his best to see that the school suffered as little as possible from the media.

'But it's all general knowledge in these parts, you know, my lord,' he said. 'Everyone's fully aware of the original assault on Moira Gale and the fact that she accused the headmaster. I'm quite sure the papers have sniffed it out; the only thing that's holding them back from hinting at a connection between the assault and the murder is the threat of libel. And it won't take them long to find a way round that—juxtaposed stories, the usual thing, I guess.'

'Yes, of course. You're quite right.' Lord Penmereth swore briefly. 'And all this just as things were beginning to look brighter. The Hilmans—the parents of that girl who got herself pregnant—they've withdrawn their complaints against the school.'

'Have they now? Why?'

'They wouldn't say at first. But I made some inquiries through another of the governors, a Mrs Carter-Black, a friend of the relation who's looking after Jane Hilman. It seems that the story the Farrow girl told you was right, Superintendent. Jane's admitted the—er—incident happened in the Easter holidays. One of those extraordinary coincidences. The man was touring, his car broke down, and oddly enough Mr Hilman took a fancy to him and suggested he stay at their house till it was repaired.'

'I—see.' Thorne spoke slowly. 'That seems a bit out of character from what people have told me of the Hilmans. Was he really a complete stranger?'

There was silence at the end of the line. Thorne stroked his moustache. He was glad Lord Penmereth couldn't see his expression. 'I need to know, sir,' he said finally, his voice cold.

'Yes, I appreciate that, Superintendent.' Lord Penmereth was a fair man, but he still hesitated. 'Would it help if I told you that the man in question has nothing to do with Coriston now?' he said. 'I can assure you that's the truth.'

'That's not quite the point, my lord,' said Thorne. 'Let's not play guessing games, sir. I take it you're referring to Simon Ford, who's just technically left the school?'

There was another pause, then, 'Yes,' replied Lord Penmereth. He had the grace to add, 'Sorry, but—'

'I know, sir. Thank you. Presumably Ford got to know the girl at Coriston—he was her maths master, after all—and they arranged the "coincidence", but I accept that none of that's my business at the moment. Unless it becomes relevant to Moira Gale's murder, you have my assurance it's forgotten. And now—'

'Yes, of course, Thorne. We're both busy men.'

Lord Penmereth took the hint at once, his voice surprisingly friendly, but the Superintendent's smile was sardonic as he put down the receiver. He got up and went to the door. 'Abbot!' he shouted, not bothering with the intercom.

'Yes, sir!' Sergeant Abbot emerged from the next office.

'Roystone's cleared of one thing, at any rate,' Thorne said. 'That teacher Simon Ford's the father of the Hilman girl's baby.'

Abbot grinned. 'Ah!' he said. 'I've got some news too. Roystone's still going to be a father. According to Dr Band, that's what made Mrs Roystone faint yesterday—that, combined with the shock of realizing her husband might be charged with murder.'

'All the more reason he shouldn't be, then,' Thorne said shortly. 'Anything else?'

'Yes, sir. A report's just come in from Reading. Our chaps have been active.' Abbot was still grinning. 'First, they've traced the jeweller where Moira got her necklet. She bought it at the beginning of July and paid cash. The shop assistant remembers her because she was so small.'

'As late as July?' Thorne grunted. 'I suppose that's not unreasonable. And?'

'They've interviewed Mr Kelsey, Moira's headmaster,' Abbot continued. 'He gave the name of the place the school party stayed at in Guernsey, and the exact dates they were there. It was a big hotel, apparently, catering for a lot of package holidays. The Guernsey police are getting a list of all their other guests during that period. Mr Kelsey also volunteered that the kids didn't always go around in one great group. Moira especially was inclined to wander off by herself.'

'So our "X" wasn't necessarily staying at the same hotel. Make them try some others—small, select ones nearby first.'

'Sir, you're sure this Guernsey trip's the connection between Moira and someone at the College?' Abbot asked tentatively; it was fairly clear what was in Thorne's mind, but it would be useful to be certain.

'Of course I'm not.' Thorne was irritable. 'They could just as easily have met in Reading, but that won't help us, and Guernsey might.'

There was a tap at the door, and a WPC opened it and peered at the Superintendent. 'Sir,' she said, 'there's a Mr Leyton—Steve Leyton—on the line. He says he understands you've been trying to get in touch with him.'

'He's right,' said Thorne without hesitation. 'Put him on. He's just the man I can do with.' To Abbot he added, 'And you go and get them to give priority to checking this Simon Ford's movements yesterday.'

The phone buzzed, and Thorne turned to it. 'Superintendent Thorne here, Mr Leyton. You're back from abroad then?'

'Yes. I flew in from Vienna last night. My father said you wanted to talk to me. I can't think why, but—'

'You were teaching at Coriston last term, Mr Leyton?'

'Yes. Oh Lord, it's not about that cannabis business, is it? It was awfully trivial.'

George Thorne smiled. Not only did Leyton have an alibi for the murder that could be checked easily, but he seemed like a frank, outspoken young man. 'Partly, but nothing for you to worry about, Mr Leyton. Tell me what happened.'

Leyton told him '. . . and that's all I know,' he concluded.

Thorne said, 'What I'm interested in is who else might have known that Pierson and Grey had been smoking pot.'

'Well, Ralph Avelon for one, but Pierson made him swear he'd never tell, and the boy's respect for Pierson was such that I think he'd keep his word. Apart from that, Pierson told me that he and Grey had kept the whole thing strictly between themselves. Superintendent, I did see them in London before I went abroad—Brigadier Pierson interviewed me for a job in a firm he's connected with—and they stuck to their story; about not having any more pot or giving any to young Avelon, I mean—'

At that moment Thorne didn't give a damn about pot-smoking schoolboys, as such. 'And what about you, Mr Leyton?' he interrupted. 'We know you didn't report the affair, but did you tell anyone—one of your colleagues, perhaps?'

'Er—yes, I did. But—oh, I suppose it doesn't matter now.'

'Mr Leyton, please don't waste any more time. Give me a direct answer. Who did you tell?'

Thorne's authority carried over the phone, and Steve Leyton responded to it. 'I'm sorry. I let it out by accident to two of the staff—Simon Ford and Paula Darby. Paula was shocked. She thought I ought to tell the head, but Simon said it was much too late to do that, and I'd only get in a mess myself. And how right he was!'

'Anyone else?'

'What? Oh, me tell anyone else? No. Definitely no. But I suppose Simon or Paula might have mentioned it. Paula's friendly with Frances Bell, but I think if Frances had known she'd have told Roystone. And—and there's always the chance that one of the other boys could have seen Pierson and Grey smoking without them knowing.' Steve Leyton was clearly puzzled. 'I don't understand why—'

'Thank you, Mr Leyton. Thank you very much.' Thorne's voice was now bland. 'You've been most helpful. I'll be in touch if I've got any more questions. You'll be at your home address for a while, will you?'

'Yes, I—'

'Good. Goodbye then, and thank you again.'

Thorne pushed back his chair and put his feet up on his desk. For some minutes he contemplated his red socks. Clever, very clever, he thought, murmuring to himself. No one could have forseen the sequence of unfortunate events—that Sylvia Roystone would have an accident and kill a child; that Jane Hilman would try for a miscarriage; that Pierson would bring cannabis back to Coriston. But each time the chance had been seized, rumours spread, action taken so that each incident had been amplified, exaggerated, worsened. Then Moira Gale and the *coup de grâce*. *Coup de grâce*, Thorne repeated to himself, pleased with the phrase.

'Sir!'

'Er—what?' Thorne, startled by Abbot's sudden entry, swung his legs off the desk.

Abbot, his mouth stretched in a wide smile, was holding out a sheet of telex paper. 'We've got him, sir. The list of visitors to that Guernsey hotel while the kids were there has just come in. Look at that third name, sir. You were right about the connection. We've got him now.'

'Mr and Mrs John Quarry,' Thorne read aloud. 'Very interesting! Obviously it's Coriston for us again this afternoon, Abbot.'

CHAPTER 23

The wrought-iron gates at the end of the drive to Coriston College were firmly closed when Thorne and Abbot drew up in front of them. Without getting out of their car the two officers could see the heavy chain and padlock which held them together.

Thorne took one look, then stretched an arm across to the steering-wheel and hooted violently. Nothing happened for several minutes, but eventually, as Thorne continued to produce staccato bursts of noise, a man in an open-necked shirt and a pair of dungarees appeared. He made no attempt to open the gates, but regarded the car sourly through the bars.

'Stop making that damned noise!' he said. 'And piss off. We've had enough bloody reporters around. And don't try sneaking in anywhere else or I'll get the police. Coriston's private property.'

'We *are* police,' Thorne snapped through the open window. 'Superintendent Thorne and Sergeant Abbot. Who are you?'

'I'm the head groundsman, when I'm not being a bloody guard.' He peered doubtfully at the warrant card that Thorne held out to him. 'Mr Roystone said—'

'I can imagine what Mr Roystone said, but keeping us waiting won't help anyone. Open those damned gates! At once!'

The man still hesitated, but Thorne's voice had conveyed authority and reluctantly he obeyed. Very slowly, to demonstrate his disapproval, he produced a key, undid the padlock, removed the chain and swung the gates open. He didn't acknowledge the 'thanks' that Abbot shouted out of the car window as he drove through.

'Mr Quarry's house, sir?' the Sergeant asked.

'Yes.' Thorne sounded vaguely regretful.

In fact, John Quarry's was one of the last names that Thorne had expected to find on the list of hotel guests. True, Quarry had a reason for wishing Roystone ill; if Roystone were forced to resign it was a near certainty that this time Lord Penmereth would get his way and see that Quarry was appointed head. But Thorne had serious reservations; this kind of motive was surely not adequate to drive a sensible man—as Quarry appeared to be—to such lengths. Besides, Thorne told himself, the characteristics of the sequence of events—the opportunities seized, the rumours spread, the use of Moira Gale, the vindictiveness behind every move, even the voice on the phone, for what that was worth—all seemed to point in one direction. More and more the Superintendent was coming to believe that Hugh Roystone's enemy was a woman. The final killing was a stumbling block, but there was no real reason why a woman, scared as well as—scorned, perhaps, shouldn't have taken the ultimate step. A woman scared as well as scorned, Thorne repeated to himself; he now had a couple of phrases to be pleased with.

He roused himself as they slowed in front of Quarry's house. Whatever his inner thoughts, there seemed a strong possibility that Mr and Mrs Quarry had been staying at the right hotel in Guernsey at the relevant time; if any problem arose—any suggestion that another couple had used the Quarrys' name—they'd have to get on to Guernsey again in search of descriptions. But he hoped—

His immediate problem was quite different. A girl in an apron, presumably a maid of some kind, appeared from the front door of the house as the car stopped. 'Can I help you?' she said politely before they had time to get out.

'Police,' Thorne said again. 'We want to speak to Mr Quarry.'

The girl eyed them with interest. 'He's not here, sir. Neither him nor Mrs Quarry. They're both over at College.

House. They've gone to lunch with the headmaster.'

'Thank you very much.' Thorne gave her his warmest smile. 'Good,' he said to Abbot. 'An ideal arrangement.'

'Yes, sir,' Abbot said neutrally as he started the car. He reflected that he hadn't the faintest idea why Thorne was so satisfied.

They found the Roystones and the Quarrys in the head-master's private garden. Frances Bell was there too; on hearing of the murder she had broken off her holiday and returned to Coriston to give what help she could. An almost empty bowl of strawberries, a collection of plates and a litter of coffee cups lay on the garden table. Until they saw Thorne the five of them looked reasonably relaxed.

'You're well guarded, Mr Roystone,' Thorne said abruptly as the headmaster rose to his feet.

'I'm sorry if you had trouble at the gate, but we're beginning to have problems with reporters. I didn't mean to hinder the police.'

'That's all right,' said Thorne, now quite cheerful. 'And good afternoon. I'm sorry too—sorry to interrupt you on such a beautiful day, but we need a little more information. Actually it was Mr Quarry we were looking for, but they told us at his house that—'

'Me? Why me?' John Quarry seemed slightly amused.

'Perhaps you'd better sit down,' Roystone said, indicating a couple more chairs on the lawn. 'I'm afraid there's no more coffee.'

'Why me?' John Quarry repeated as Thorne and Abbot arranged themselves. This time his query sounded a little tentative.

'Because I'd like to ask about your Easter holidays earlier this year. Where did you and Mrs Quarry spend them?'

'You would, would you?' Quarry's amusement had now quite faded. 'It's none of your bloody business,' he said with surprising roughness, 'but in fact Helen and I went to the

States. It was a trip we'd been planning for some time. It was terrific,' he added more pleasantly. 'We hope to go again soon.'

'I see,' said Thorne. 'Then at no time during last April were you in the Channel Isles—in Guernsey, for example?'

For a few moments there was silence, broken only by a sharp intake of breath from one of the women. Thorne, watching John Quarry, wasn't sure which. Roystone had knocked a coffee cup off the table on to the grass, and was taking his time picking it up.

'No, I—I've never been to Guernsey in my life,' Quarry said at last, quite calmly. 'Why do you ask, Superintendent?'

'Why? Because—' Thorne paused and looked around the group, his eyes moving slowly from one face to the next. 'Why? Because I'm investigating the death—the murder—of a young girl, and I expect help from all responsible members of the public.'

There was an appreciable pause before Quarry answered. 'I know that, Superintendent, but I fail to see any connection between the Gale girl and my Easter vacation. Anyway, I've given you my answer.'

'You've given me *an* answer, yes, sir. Would you like to change it?' Thorne asked without apparent emotion. 'Perhaps before you reply I should tell you that Moira Gale was herself in Guernsey at that time, and it's probable that there she met the individual who later paid her to accuse Mr Roystone of assault and attempted rape.'

'But, good God, you can't think I had anything to do with—'

'You can't imagine that John—'

'You mean you've got evidence that Hugh's innocent—'

Thorne ignored the protests, and Hugh Roystone stayed silent too. He sat, staring at the remains of lunch on the table, his knuckles white, his mouth set.

'John, dear, we must tell them.' It was Helen who spoke quite quietly, once the chorus had subsided.

Thorne said, 'That's excellent advice, Mrs Quarry. It may take a little time, but it won't be difficult to check the facts. If anyone from Coriston was in Guernsey at the same time as Moira Gale it's ten to one they were seen together by someone somewhere.'

'Maybe, but it damn well wasn't me!' John Quarry exploded. 'To my knowledge I've never set eyes on that girl—in Guernsey or anywhere else.'

'However, you were in Guernsey at Easter, sir?'

'They went to the United States,' Frances Bell said. 'They told us all about it at the beginning of term—how much they'd enjoyed it and—'

'No, Frances. We didn't go to the States. We had intended to, but—' Helen Quarry looked at her husband. 'Will you explain, John, or must I?'

'Oh, I will,' Quarry said acidly. 'If you want to know, the truth is we couldn't afford it. It was all planned, but we've got a damn fool of an extravagant son-in-law. He wrote a large cheque that bounced. It was a question of finding the money or seeing him prosecuted—perhaps sent to prison for fraud. For the sake of our daughter we decided we couldn't allow that. So the trip to the States had to be sacrificed. We stayed with Helen's aunt for a while, but that was rather tedious and a short cheap package holiday in Guernsey seemed a good idea. Unfortunately we'd only been there a couple of days when the hotel was invaded by a crowd of schoolchildren—presumably including Moira Gale.' He looked inquiringly at the Superintendent.

'Thank you, sir,' Thorne said. 'We'll have to check the dates, but—'

'Oh, Helen, I'm so sorry.' Frances Bell put out a hand.

'As to why we lied about it,' Quarry went on, 'that was my foolish idea, not Helen's, but everyone else always seems able to afford such wonderful holidays, and having made so much of our plans beforehand I wasn't prepared to admit we'd cancelled them—especially for that reason. Now you know.'

'It's very understandable, sir,' Thorne said. He turned to Abbot. 'Sergeant, before we go, get on the blower and see if there's anything new in at Kidlington.'

'What next?' Frances Bell demanded as Abbot went off to their car and the radio.

Thorne shrugged. 'More work for the police, Miss Bell. There's always a lot of checking to be done in cases like this, here at Coriston and in Colombury, in Reading, and of course in Guernsey—especially in Guernsey. Then gradually the bits start to fit a pattern, till the irrelevancies can be ignored and the truth becomes clear—'

'It's not clear yet, then?' Hugh Roystone said.

This was the first time the headmaster had spoken for some time, and Thorne gave him an apologetic smile. 'No, Mr Roystone, I'm afraid not. But it will be soon, sir, we hope. For your sake.'

Roystone gave the Superintendent a curious look and nodded. Abbot had returned and he handed Thorne a note. Thorne unfolded it and read, 'Mrs Hugh Roystone at a small hotel close by. Roystone expected but didn't show.' Slowly Thorne folded it again and put it in the top pocket of his jacket, disregarding the interested eyes that were fixed on him.

'Thanks, Abbot,' he said. 'And many thanks to you all. You must excuse us now.' He was on his feet and making for the exit from the garden before they realized he was going.

'Hurry, Abbot! Get a move on!' Thorne said as soon as they were out of earshot.

'Why, sir? And where to?' Abbot didn't often question his superior so directly, but for once he felt really naked. So far, he believed he'd followed Thorne's line of reasoning and had reached the same conclusion. Now he was suddenly completely at a loss. 'Where to?' he repeated.

'To pay a call on Roystone's former mistress, Abbot. Haven't you ever heard of a woman scorned—the fury of

a woman scorned? The last straw must have been when
she found that Roystone preferred his wife to her. Mrs
Roystone's a nice girl, but no one would call her an
efficient, forceful character.'

'I know that, sir, but—but I thought Frances Bell—'

'Oh no, Abbot. Not Miss Bell. She's efficient all right, and
she may have a soft spot for Roystone, but I can't see her as
his discarded girlfriend. I'm sure he wasn't thinking of her
when we threw him by mentioning Guernsey—especially
further inquiries there.'

'Then who, sir?'

'Think, Abbot! Who suggested that Sylvia Roystone
should take that minibus to fetch those lads from the station
at the beginning of term? Our woman can't have known what
would happen, of course, but she might have done a bit of
wishful thinking, perhaps. And who was around when Betty
Farrow fell over that broken gin bottle? Who sent Jane
Hilman to fetch a book from a room where more gin was
conveniently on view? Who was one of those in an ideal
position to start rumours? Who knew about Pierson's cannabis and could easily have put more in his study? And who
always took a sensible line in any crisis, but let herself and
her views be overridden? And who had planned to leave
Coriston at the end of their summer term?'

'You mean—'

'Yes, Abbot. Unless I'm much mistaken, Miss Paula
Darby. Let's get over to her cottage at Fairfield, and see
what's happening. Who knows, Hugh Roystone might be
along too.'

CHAPTER 24

Thorne and Abbot found Auburn Cottage about half a mile outside the village of Fairfield. It was a small, modern house, but it had been built of the cream-coloured stone that is characteristic of the Cotswolds. Set back from the road, in the lee of a hill on the edge of Fairfield Wood, Auburn Cottage was both sheltered and secluded. The two police officers drove slowly past. From the road the place looked deserted, but a car was parked outside the garage.

'Stop here!' the Superintendent said suddenly to Abbot.

The road had curved to the left and they were able to draw up on the grass verge, well out of sight of the cottage. They walked back a few hundred yards before entering the wood, and then moved cautiously through the trees until they reached a gate set in a hedge that was clearly a side boundary of Miss Darby's property. Open french windows at the rear of the house could be seen across a small, neat lawn.

'I'll watch the garden,' Thorne said softly. 'We can always go in through those windows if we need to. Lucky the hedge is thick enough to give some cover. You go on round, Abbot, so that you can see the front. Get back here as soon as Roystone arrives.'

'*If* he arrives, sir. He might phone.'

'With his wife there—and Frances Bell? I doubt if he'd risk it. No. He'll come himself. He's got to talk to her. He's got to know whether what he's guessing at is true. He can't just sit and hope. There's too much at stake so far as he's concerned.' Thorne gave a mirthless grin. 'No, Abbot, he'll come.'

But as time passed and Roystone made no appearance, the Superintendent began to have his own doubts. It was hot under the trees and midges bit him. He tried sitting on the ground, but found the hedge was thicker still at its base and impeded his view. He stood first on one leg, then on the other. Fiercely he stroked his moustache. In his mind he had a picture of Hugh Roystone driving rapidly in quite a different direction to see quite a different woman—some woman whose name hadn't yet been mentioned in connection with the case. Or of course he might still be idling in his garden with his wife and friends calmly finishing off his damned strawberries.

'No, no,' Thorne muttered to himself. Basically he was right, he was sure of it. Just as he'd expected, Roystone had reacted to the reference to Guernsey with dismay and sudden understanding. The headmaster had no option but to confirm or refute what he dreaded. There was no way he could remain in doubt. The only question was the identity of the woman.

Minutes later Paula Darby came through the french windows on to the lawn, carrying a blanket and obviously intent on basking in the sun. She was wearing a halter top and the briefest of shorts, so that her excellent figure was clearly displayed. Her skin was bronzed, her fair hair shone and— Thorne guessed—her eyes were blue. She looked confident and capable. Yet, strangely enough, there was a distinct resemblance to Sylvia Roystone. George Thorne was re-assured that he was right; he even felt he could begin to understand why Roystone had rejected this obviously positive woman in favour of someone less assertive.

Thorne's ears caught the sound of an approaching car and, minutes later, after Paula Darby had gone back into the cottage, Abbot was at his side. 'He's come, sir. Mr Roystone's arrived. Not too welcome either, from what I could see, but she's let him in—a girl in a suntop and shorts.'

'I know. Good!' Thorne didn't mind showing his satisfac-tion. 'So now we'll try a spot of eavesdropping if we can. Come along. The gate's not locked, but tread carefully.'

He led the way, through the gate and along a short path, to stand by the back wall of the cottage next to the french windows. He motioned to Abbot to stay beside him. Neither of them had any difficulty in hearing what was being said inside the room. Hugh Roystone and Paula Darby were making no effort to keep their voices down.

'. . . just using me. Always promising a wedding, weren't you, Hugh? But it never materialized. I should have realized from all the trouble you took to make sure no one had a clue about us. And God knows that was hard enough in that bloody hothouse you run. When I think of Frances Bell, trying to poke her damned nose into our business, I could bloody well scream—'

'Paula, I told you. I thought we should be sure—'

'Sure! For God's sake, how long does it take to be sure? You made your mind up soon enough about that bitch Sylvia, didn't you? I suppose it was the only way to get her into bed. Though why you should want a pallid little piece like her when—'

Thorne and Abbot glanced at each other; they couldn't see into the room, but they were both simultaneously visualizing Paula Darby comparing herself and her appearance with Sylvia's.

'Leave Sylvia out of this, Paula!'

'Why? If it hadn't been for her, you'd have joined me in Guernsey and we'd have been going on as usual now. Right now, probably. God, how I hate you, Hugh!' Paula Darby's voice rose. 'She's not worth hating. But you! How the hell do you think I felt at that cosy little hotel? They all remembered us from our other visits, of course. Everyone called me Mrs Roystone and kept asking when you were coming. Then that bloody letter of yours. So sorry. Can't come. Just got married. Have the deeds of the cottage instead—a wedding present the wrong way round. Appealed to your sense of humour, did it?'

'What else could I say except I was sorry?'

'You didn't even have the guts to tell me to my face!'

'I didn't have the chance.'

'Well, I swore then you'd pay for it, Hugh, and you have. I've ruined you professionally, even if you keep out of gaol. Old Penmereth'll never let you stay on at your beloved Coriston, not after all those jolly little happenings last term, and now—'

'So it was you—everything that went wrong.'

'Not quite everything. I didn't get Jane Hilman pregnant, for one thing. That was Simon Ford's effort—his very own contribution. But I seized my chances, and did a little rumour-mongering. I expect Penmereth showed you the anonymous letter about you and small fair girls—Betty Farrow gave me that idea.'

'You're crazy, Paula. Do you know that? You're crazy!' There was disgust in Roystone's voice. Then his tone changed as he remembered. 'And Moira Gale? You arranged that too?'

'The assault on your virtue? Yes. I arranged that all right. To tell the truth, I was getting a bit worried; it looked as if you might survive, after all. I came across the stupid little girl in Guernsey—while I was waiting for you, Hugh. Quite appropriate, wasn't it? I gave her a lift one day and we met quite often on the island. I got to know her well, talking about books and Bronson's shop, and how she wanted to better herself. When I needed someone I thought of her—I guessed she'd do anything for money. I went to Reading and got hold of her just before the end of term, as soon as I knew when you'd be coming back from your silly conference. I told the girl my husband had been playing around and I wanted to get my own back. It wasn't hard to work out when she should be on the road, and your car's unmistakable, quite apart from the number. I know it was a pretty thin story, but I thought a fifteen-year-old would swallow it. I misjudged her.'

'I said you were mad, Paula. In any case it would have been her word against mine—'

'I know, but mud sticks, Hugh. Anyway, we were lucky. She couldn't have chosen a better moment, could she, with those butchers—what were they called, Ingle?—as witnesses.'

'And suppose they hadn't come along?'

'Moira was to escape from your clutches as best she could, and run to her aunt, crying rape—or assault, at least. And she knew who you were, remember? That was important. We discussed the plan carefully.'

'But, Paula, you were putting yourself in the girl's hands—'

'So what? She wasn't likely to go to the police. Did you know the silly little bitch had the most ridiculous pretentious delusions? She knew she'd been adopted, and she'd come to think she had royal connections, or some such nonsense. The last thing she wanted was publicity that might hurt her stupid name in the future. And I paid her well.'

'Still, Paula—a child like that—How could—'

But there was no stopping Paula now. 'Besides, I thought she only knew me as Mrs Roystone, like everyone else on that damned island. That's what I meant when I said I misjudged her. It wasn't till she telephoned me here and demanded more that I discovered she'd been alone in my room at that hotel one day while I went to the loo, and she'd opened my bag and found my real name—'

'So that was it—you *were* in her hands. She could have gone on blackmailing you. Or in spite of her pretentions she might have told her story—for the money, maybe. Perhaps if you'd got to Australia in time you'd have been safe from the police, but I'd have been off the hook too. So you had to kill her. And you tried to involve me.'

'Sure she had to die. And as for involving you—why not? It might have worked. And I'd nothing to lose.'

'You bloody woman! How I could ever—' Hugh Roystone's voice rose in anger, and Thorne waited no longer. With a gesture to Abbot he took a pace forward and stepped over the sill of the french windows.

'Miss Darby? Paula Darby?'

'Who the hell are you?'

'Police, Miss Darby. Superintendent Thorne and Sergeant Abbot, Thames Valley Serious Crimes Squad. Miss Darby, I—'

Superintendent Thorne, to Abbot's great relief, proceeded to give Paula Darby the official warning, but she paid him no attention. She had turned on Hugh Roystone.

'Damn you!' she said. 'So it was all a trap. You brought the police. I should have expected it. It's the sort of thing you would do. You always were a moral coward. God knows why I ever loved you!'

'Miss Darby, I must ask you to come with us to Kidlington police station where you'll—'

'Yes. All right.' Paula seemed scarcely interested in Thorne's words. 'Just let me get some clothes on.'

Hugh Roystone stood back as the Sergeant ushered Paula Darby from the room. The adrenalin engendered by her confession had ceased to flow, leaving him emotionally drained. He sank back into a chair and stared sightlessly at the ceiling of the sunlit room. Then he lowered his eyes to meet Thorne's, his expression a curious mixture of dismay and relief.

The Superintendent had the last words. 'A few hours ago I was thinking of fury—the fury of a woman scorned,' he said. 'Go home to your wife and your school, Mr Roystone. There'll be a trial and the media'll make a meal of it, but with luck you'll all three survive. You've been more fortunate than Moira Gale.'

There was nothing Roystone could do but bow his head.